I0567722

Sci Crew
Beyond the Horizon

by Anthony Gordon Bennett

Sci Crew

Beyond the Horizon

by Anthony Gordon Bennett

Printed in the United States of America
Published by Blue Orb Books,
McLean, VA
www.BlueOrbBooks.com
Library of Congress Number 2013956576

Cover illustration by: Edward Rowan
Special thanks to: Diana, Leslie, Jack, Mike, Nico, John, Tom, Janet, and Erik.

CHAPTER 1

November, 2017   New York, New York

The world economy had tanked again. Once again, a few of the über wealthy had twisted things and profited as the lot for the rest grew bleak. In retrospect, it was always amazing how few it took to muck things up. One pebble in a shoe.

It was one thing when everyone knew times were tough and pulled together. It was quite another when there was acrimony and blame.

Young Charlie Leake, strong, handsome, and smart, lay in bed listening to his parents fight. Or rather his father would say something and his mother would yell. His father's favorite saying, "Snow and rain", meant that during the winter everyone was happy because you could go sledding and during the spring it would rain, the crops would be bountiful and everyone could eat. "The Earth always takes care of us, even when it looks cold and dark. There is a natural rhythm to the universe. Always be positive." It was good advice.

His father had said this when he was a successful corporate manager. His mother had always hated that expression, but more so now that his dad had been trying to start a business for the past several years which wasn't going well. No one's business was going well. "Get a job," he heard her say for the thousandth time.

Being positive sounds good, but it doesn't pay the bills, he thought. He vowed never to be poor, no matter what he had to do. He repeated that to himself every day over the next several years.

CHAPTER 2

January, 2030   Davos, Switzerland

Davos is the site of the World Economic Forum's annual meeting. Corporate CEOs, heads of state, top scientists, and leading academics gather to facilitate solutions to the top global issues of the day. This meeting had been occurring for decades, mostly in an advisory capacity. But now, business leaders rose up the ranks based on the number of people their products helped, and political dynasties had gone away, individuals that viewed science and technology as a way to solve world problems came to power. Collectively, the members of the Forum were a force for good and once they voted, things got accomplished.

The president of the WEF, Walter Einstein, winner of a Nobel Prize in Physics and a distant cousin of Alfred, opened the conference.

"Ladies and gentlemen, thank you for attending this year's conference. As you know, we have made great strides in bringing the world together, making us all feel more unified. Our first vote since *The Incident,* was to eliminate nuclear weapons altogether and replace nuclear power plants with renewables."

There was great applause from the attendees.

"Over the past few years we have also voted unanimously on several major items. We voted to have all our countries speak English…"

More applause.

This had been an easy vote as essentially everyone already spoke English. For decades all air traffic control and pilots had been required to speak English. Most international business transactions were conducted in English. And the world had embraced American movies and television. It also made economic sense as it eliminated costly translations and duplicate printing.

"To have all our countries go metric…"

Additional cheering.

America had been the only non-metric country for years. The Metric Board had tried to get the U.S. to switch over in the 1970s, but was beaten back by corporations that thought it would be too expensive. Once digital machinery came about, the conversion was simple. U.S. exports actually went up and industry was embarrassed that they had dragged their feet.

"To have all our countries drive on the right side of the road…"

Everyone applauded except for English Prime Minister Goodall, a great grandson of the primatologist Jane Goodall.

"Come on Goodall," exhorted Einstein, "you know it worked out for the best."

Over two hundred thousand troops, construction workers, and road crews from around the world had descended on England and switched over the road signs and traffic lights in one day as the citizens remained off the street for that day.

Goodall slowly applauded and the rest applauded even harder.

"And last year we voted to have all our countries adopt a unified financial system based on World Monetary Units, or WUs as they've come to be called."

Cheers and applause.

"This year we will discuss the measure to catch computer hackers within hours, and sentence them to life in prison with only crayons and wax paper on which to communicate with."

Stunned silence from the attendees.

"Just kidding. Making sure you were all awake. This year we will discuss the measure to eliminate illiteracy, and how to finance over one million teachers to fan out around the globe to teach children and adults to read and write."

This was a popular measure and there was wild cheering and applause.

Off to the side of the hall stood Dr. Walstib, one of the most respected scientists in the world, and now its richest person. He had made his trillions by inventing an extremely efficient and yet low cost solar panel. His was the brand that the world had adopted when the measure was voted on to replace nuclear power with renewables. He was surrounded by three Presidents: President Filho of Brazil, a relative of Carlos Chagas Filho former president of the Brazilian Academy of Sciences; President Tereshkova of Russia, a relative of Valentina Vladimirovna Tereshkova the first female in space; and President Meng of China, a relative of Ling Meng the famous plant biologist.

Dr. Walstib had become friends with many heads of state as he personally supervised much of the installation of millions of solar panels in the major countries. He leaned over to his friends and whispered, "I for one would vote for that hacker proposal."

The three presidents laughed and nodded in agreement.

Charles Leake stood in the back of the hall by himself. He was now the twentieth richest person in the world. He had started out buying up small parking lots and adding electric outlets for the booming electric car market. His lots became popular and he leveraged those assets to buy parking garages. He then leveraged those to buy office buildings. He then went vertical to purchase cement and iron companies to build new office buildings. He worked hard and was resentful of those richer than he who had gotten rich through inventions. He thought most of their creations were a matter of luck and discounted the thousands of hours inventors spent in the lab.

Einstein continued, "Before we hear specifics on the literacy measure, we have a special guest speaker. Dr. Fissile is here to update us on the storage programs instituted for the nuclear material removed from the weapons and power facilities."

CHAPTER 3

May, 2032   Washington, DC

The room was quiet. The entire building was quiet. Only the soft tick of the government-issue analog clock on the wall could be heard. Then, the loud screech of the buzzer ripped through the room.

Neil had hit the buzzer a tenth of a second before his teammates and three tenths of a second before the opposing team. The audience was anxious, but their concern was moot. Neil's answer, "Precambrian", was, of course, correct. The question had been: "The cores of modern continents, called cratons, were formed mainly during the: Paleozoic, Phanerozoic, Precambrian, or Mesozoic period?" The four teammates looked at each other with a combination of happiness and relief. The parents and teachers and friends in the audience from Steve Jobs High School cheered wildly. The scoreboard on the wall behind them said it all, Steve Jobs High School (California) 201 points – Thomas Jefferson High School (Virginia) 199 points.

They hugged their parents briefly, then their teacher sponsor showed them out into the hallway where a barrage of camera crews and reporters had been waiting.
The closest reporter, an attractive young woman with blonde hair, shoved a microphone at them and asked, "This is the first time that four freshmen have won the US

Department of Science's National Science Quiz Bowl.
Anne, Ellie, Neil, and Yang, how do you feel?"
Smiles, nervous laughter, and deep sighs were their only
answers.
The reporter looked at the camera and said, "Well they are
obviously happy!" Then looked back at the winning team,
and asked, "Which of the prizes will you pick?"
They looked at each other and shrugged. Anne could only
muster, "We don't know yet."
The reporter, having done her homework, tried to shift the
interview to a personal approach. "I understand each of you
was named after an eminent scientist. Neil, I gather you
were named after Neil Armstrong, the first person on
Earth's moon?"
Neil looked at her and said, "Yes."
She moved the microphone over and asked, "Anne, you
were named after Anna Lee Fisher, an astronaut, an MD,
and mother of the year in 1984?"
Anne smiled back and said, "Yes."
The reporter smiled, urging her on.
Anne continued, "My parents hoped I'd be interested in
science if I had the name as a connection. I guess it
worked."
The reporter seemed satisfied and moved on. "Ellie, I
understand you were named after Ellen Ochoa, the first
Hispanic astronaut?"
Ellie smiled, "Well I don't know if I'll become an
astronaut, but I admire her and hope I can work on
something useful to mankind."

"Excellent," said the reporter as she shifted to Yang.
"Yang, I see from my research that you were named after
Yang Liwei, the first Chinese astronaut?"
"I sure was," beamed Yang. "He was a hero and someday I
hope to follow in his footsteps."
The reporter hoped she was getting the winning teammates
into the rhythm of the interview and started to ask another
question.
However, the team began to move away and back to their
parents.
The reporter looked back at the camera, her perky smile
almost masking the sarcasm in her voice said, "There you
have it. They gave it their all and are too exhausted to
answer another question."

The team, sensed they were being dissed by a reporter who
hadn't gotten the interview-of-the-year, turned back to the
reporter. Yang signaled for the reporter to come over. She
perked up again and held up her microphone.
Yang looked directly at the reporter, and in a very serious
voice said, "For the last year we spent every free moment
learning about science because it's exciting and important.
We concentrated on the task at hand which was winning
this science tournament, which we did. We are elated. We
allowed ourselves a little time to think about the prize
options. We think we'd like to go to Africa to study
elephant herd migration patterns."
Her TV smile turned genuine, and she said to Yang, "Good
choice." The reporter turned back to the camera, "This is
Mary Lanta signing off from the National Science Quiz

Bowl." She put down the mic and the cameraperson turned off the camera.

Mary said softly to Yang, "Sorry. I didn't mean to be pushy. It's just that I love science. It's my beat, and I get tired of the whole shy scientist thing. The world needs to know more about what you all are doing and accomplishing."

Yang responded, "We didn't mean to be standoffish. We just didn't know your intentions. We'd like to talk more but we have to go. We'll owe you one."

They turned and headed back to their parents.

Yang looked back at the reporter who was still looking at him. He gave her a big smile.

Neil looked at Yang, "Give it a rest."

"I'm just being polite," protested Yang.

CHAPTER 4

December, 2032

Charlie Leake, sitting alone in a very luxurious apartment is staring at a wall of video monitors paying no attention to the beautiful view of New York City 150 stories below. The wall of screens showed various financial charts from around the world including the U.S. Stock Exchange, the Euro Stock Exchange, the African Stock Exchange, the Asian Stock Exchange, and the South American Stock Exchange. In addition there were several smaller, more detailed screens showing information about Leake industries, and four TV monitors each showing talking heads discussing financial news.

TV screens one, two, and four went silent and screen three flashed a message on the screen along with a subtle male computer voice reading the message, "Selected key words detected".

The message stopped scrolling and the two financial talking heads on screen three reappeared. Despite the fact that it was a financial network, the anchor persons were selected, in part, for their looks.

Cassidy, beautiful with flowing red hair, looked at her co-anchor, "Thanks Bobby, great statistics. And now we go to… Wait, I'm being told we just received the news we've been waiting for."

Bobby, tall and handsome with thick dark brown hair, looked admiringly at his co-anchor and asked, "What is it Cassidy?"

She looked back at the camera, "This just in. As you know, Smart Mart Financial tracks the wealthiest individuals around the world and their latest rankings have just been released. We have them for you here exclusively on Global Financial News Daily."

"Always exciting," chimed in Bobby, still looking fondly at Cassidy.

"Let's start at number 10. Moving up from number 12 is Charlie Leake, head of Leake Industries."

"Oh, he's ruthless."

"Tough but fair, is what I've heard," said Cassidy as she looked straight at the TV studio camera and batted her eyes.

"And still single?" said Bobby trying not to sound jealous.

"Why yes, yes I believe he is," said Cassidy, while she still starred at the camera.

"Why does he go by Mr. Charlie instead of Mr. Leake?" Bobby inquired, now sounding a little sarcastic.

"He tells people he's just a simple southern gentleman."

"No he's not. He's an MBA type from New York City," said Bobby with contempt.

"I think he's just fine," said Cassidy beaming into the camera.

"Moving on, let's hear about number nine," said Bobby, still slightly flustered.

The TV audio muted as the com-system buzzed and a phone number and name flashed on one of the blank screens.

"Accept," said Leake.

A woman's face appeared on the screen. All the other screens faded to black.

"Hi Mom."

"Hi Sweetie. I just saw the news. Number ten. Congratulations. Did you see it?"

"Yes."

"You know I was just a little bitty upset last year when you were only number twelve."

"I remember you saying that."

"Well number ten is really something."

"I've been working hard."

"I gather. We never see you."

"I've been working hard."

"Well, what about next year? Do you think you could be in the top five?"

Short lived glory, he thought.

"Maybe. I'm working on a new project."

"You already do so many things. Mining, construction, manufacturing, apartments."

"I have to move out of what's moving down and move into what's moving up."

"So tell me about the new project."

"Not yet, but I think it could leap-frog me into the number one spot."

"Then I'd really be happy."

I doubt it, he thought. "Gotta run Mom. Bye."

"Bye Sweetie."

The screen went blank.

"Resume all screens," said Leake.

They all popped back on and were aglow with charts and statistics.

Sci Crew

He stared at the screens and smiled to himself.

CHAPTER 5

June, 2035   Sonoran Desert, Arizona

A spectacular building stood tall in the Arizona desert, comprised of two towers that held a massive wind turbine in the middle. The whole building turned gently to catch the wind. It was encircled by thousands of solar panels.

Just outside the ring of solar panels, the sand shook slightly. A strip of desert about one hundred meters long by thirty meters wide suddenly lowered about one meter then slid sideways. A metal launch ramp, angled slightly upward at the far end, raised up. Without a sound, a long sleek black fuselage with short wings shot out. The launch ramp lowered and the launch ramp canopy slid back into place. Once airborne, the scramjets kicked in and the plane shot forward at an amazing speed. The plane reached an altitude of ten kilometers within seconds.

The pilot looked out at a beautiful view of the southern desert and mountains. His voice, steady and calm, "So peaceful… What fabulous views of this little part of the world…Maybe a little soothing test flight music." The pilot pushed a few buttons, and the cockpit was filled with 'The Wheels on the Bus', decidedly not soothing.

The pilot pushed a button and the music stopped.

"Jimmy?" said the pilot's voice into the com-system, still calm.

Jim Row, the chief technical expert for the HyperRider, the world's fastest scramjet, responded, his voice coming from the com-system, "Sorry, Sir. Mae put me up to it."

The pilot said, slightly amused, "Kids. How many times have I told her not to mess with Daddy's scramjet?"

Jim's voice, "She's eighteen now, Sir. Maybe she's trying to tell you something. Anyway, push the button again and you'll be back to your music."

The pilot said, "Thanks. Everything's running stable. Heading north. We're at Mach 10. Making a turn to the west. Smooth turn."

The plane is cutting through the clouds at unbelievable speed.

"We're at Mach 17."

"The numbers are looking good here," said Jim.

The sound barrier, 1225 kilometers per hour, or Mach 1, was initially called a barrier because airplane engineers believed that no plane could pass that speed without breaking apart. Propellers could only move a plane so fast and thus jet engines were developed. The first level flight, rather than a steep dive, to break the barrier took place in 1947. Improvements were gradual until culminating in the SR-71 spy plane which, in 1964, achieved Mach 3. Scramjets were the next step and achieved Mach 5 in 2013.

"Uh, oh. There's a massive storm coming from the north heading down the coast. I'm making a U-turn, heading south along the coast."

"As long as you're heading south, why don't you go visit Mae? It'll only take a few minutes. You've been up here working on this project a long time."

"It is flying smoothly. Yes, that's a good idea. Thank you."

The pilot pushed the button and a very pleasing 'Eyes of the World' filled the cabin. The HyperRider turned slightly to the southeast, and held steady at Mach 17.

CHAPTER 6

June, 2035

It's not often a group of fifth graders is very, very quiet.
But today, in the back study room of the library in the Bill
Gates Elementary School, everyone listened attentively to
Yang. Yang, Chinese, handsome and athletic with a shock
of spiky black hair, was their math tutor. He had been
taking Advanced Placement and International
Baccalaureate math classes since the fifth grade. Yang's
students had all been handpicked by their teachers
throughout the county for their ability to move forward
quickly in mathematics.

Yang had a big grin on his face as he finished the lesson.
"I'm so proud of you all. This is the seventh time that each
of you has received one hundred percent on your weekly
exam. This school year has been amazing, and I look
forward to tutoring you all throughout the summer. Next
week we will concentrate on radius, diameter, and
circumference. But as always, before we do the numbers,
ask the important questions. Why are we learning this?
What are the practical applications? Over the weekend
research what a low resistance tire, a parabolic mirror, and
the earth have in common. Have a fun weekend and I'll see
you next week."

One of the students in the front row received a couple of
nudges from adjacent students and he then raised his hand
while at the same time asking his question. "Mr. Yang, we
are curious. Now that you've graduated, what will you be
doing this summer?" Yang, paused for a moment before

answering seriously, "Well, mostly some research and getting ready to go off to college." He grinned again and added, "But tonight, as I've done every Friday night the last four years, I will join my three best friends for a little surfing."

Not far away at the Fowler Elephant Rehabilitation Center, Ellie, a stunning Hispanic girl with dark brown hair and a beautiful smile, was helping Dr. Fowler, the zoo veterinarian. The vet was filing one nail on the foot of a small, old elephant while Ellie stroked the elephant's trunk and fed it apples.

As the vet filed, she talked with Ellie, "I can't believe how much easier this task is since you changed things around. This used to be a long tedious chore and we would end up sedating the elephants almost every time, which just can't be good for them in the long run."

Ellie tried to keep from beaming as she responded, "Thank you. I almost didn't mention anything when I first saw how the nail trimmings were scheduled. My mom kept telling me to sit back, learn the ropes, listen, and learn."

The vet chimed in, "Generally that is good advice." Ellie demurred, "True. But it seemed that scheduling all the nails to be trimmed at once was based on making it easier for the staff. Once I read about behavior reward theory, it made sense to look at the task from the elephant's point of view. A small task, such as one toe nail, that gets a big reward, such as an apple, would yield compliant, even willing, behavior." The vet nodded, "And we can certainly fit in filing one nail, a five minute task, almost any time, even if we have to do it several days in a row. This actually makes

scheduling easier. With a happy animal it only takes two of us. There, all done. Speaking of scheduling, your shift is done. Next time, would you like to try the filing?"
Ellie gave the elephant one more pat. "Yes, I'd love to. Thank you Dr. Fowler. See you next week."

Tall, blonde, and with a swimmer's body, Anne stood on the deck of the pool talking with her new group of scuba volunteers, mostly retirees. "I hope you enjoyed your first day of in-water training."
An older man in the back interrupted, "When do we get to go in the ocean?"
Anne smiled, "Soon. I'm glad you are enthusiastic. You all obviously passed the written exam. And now you've completed the first day of in-water training and gotten your feet wet."
A few laughs.
"Lame, I know. I've got to get a better joke writer. This first day I merely got you familiar with your gear. Next week you will get more familiar with actually using the equipment in various mock settings in the pool. You will practice re-introducing coral, planting kelp, and feeding fish. Best to be completely familiar with your equipment before we place you in cold, dark, fast moving ocean currents."
The group looked horrified.
"Just kidding. You will be wearing warm drysuits. You will be tethered. And during the initial phase, your ocean floor zone will be well lit. Any more questions?"
The group, now assured, was all smiles.

"This is important work. I am delighted that you, and the thousands of others around the world, have volunteered to help the Ocean Re-stocking Program. Thank you. I look forward to seeing you next week."

Yang, Ellie, and Anne each walked quickly out of their respective buildings. Each gave a quick look at their watches as they dropped into the seat of their Tryx, their handmade electric three-wheeled motorcycles. Silently and quickly they each left their parking lots, made a few turns, found their way to Wilshire Boulevard, and headed west. After a few minutes they each arrived at Pacific Coast Highway and headed north. Within minutes they found themselves in a mini-convoy enjoying the salty breeze as they surged gracefully along the winding road. They pulled into the parking lot on the ocean side of the street and parked next to another electric three-wheeled motorcycle that was already parked. Once they had parked, the license plates could be read in order, SciTeam1, SciTeam2, SciTeam3, and SciTeam4.

CHAPTER 7

Bill's Beach Shack had been there forever, the ocean blue
paint was mostly faded and the main color now seemed to
be touches of gray primer. Bill's catered to surfers, as
attested to by the sign out front:

> No Reservations – No Surfing
> No Surfing – No Reservations

Yang, Ellie, and Anne walked in the front door. On one
side was floor to ceiling windows that overlooked the
ocean and the other walls were covered with surf pictures
and flip-flops.

They were greeted warmly by Bill, "Neil said to send you
down to the board lockers. No worries, I've got your table
reserved."

They walked outside and down the side stairs to the beach.
Under the overhanging first floor of the restaurant was a
row of tall slender surfboard lockers. A few empty locker
doors were open, as the locker owners were out surfing.

Neil, tall and muscular, with long, curly blonde hair, stood
in front of their four lockers with a huge grin, "I made us a
graduation present." Neil was the team expert in physics
and engineering and could design and build almost
anything.

Ellie blushed and said softly, "You shouldn't have."

Yang blurted out, "Sure he shoulda. Where are they?"

"Open your lockers," said Neil.

They each placed their forefinger on the fingerprint locks,
opened the doors, and pulled out their surfboards. The

boards looked normal other than the newly embedded small wires on the top and the small grooves on the bottom. "This is amazing!" said Anne, "This looks like a photovoltaic grid on the top surface. But what is this underneath?"

Neil pointed, "The front grooves house the intake vents and the back grooves house the ejector nozzles. The small hump in the middle is an electric impeller motor juiced by the solar panel now imbedded on the top of your boards. And here is the on-off switch imbedded on top."

Yang was smiling, "So we jet out to the waves instead of having to paddle out. That is so Alva bro. Thanks."

Ellie gave Neil a big hug.

They grinned at each other for a second, then grabbed their swimsuits out of the lockers, and ran into the changing rooms. Thirty-seven seconds later they were back in front of their lockers. "Let's ride," they said in unison. They grabbed their boards, ran down to the beach, headed into the water, and jetted out to the waves.

The waves were spectacular, about two meters and glassy. This was the best surfing they had had in months.

After a few sets Neil looked at his watch then shouted to the others, "Let's rest a few minutes."

Yang was quick to say, "With these new boards we aren't tired, we don't need to rest, let's keep surfing."

Neil looked at his watch again, "I know, let's just sit a bit."

Anne quipped, "Sit-a-bit, sounds like a new medicine. Take two sit-a-bit and call me in the morning."

They sat on their boards and bobbed gently in the waves.

Ellie asked, "So Neil, where did you make the adjustments to the boards?"

Neil wiped the water from his face, "In the Tech Lab at school."

Ellie was surprised, "Mr. Garcia lets you still use the lab?"

Neil looked at his watch, "Well, I have been going in there for a week now to clean the lab up, and he just let me keep working on stuff."

Yang interrupted, "Dude you know school's over and you don't have to clean up anymore."

Neil looked straight at Yang, "It's not the cleaning up that's important, it's the next project."

Ellie chimed in, "Another project? More than these boards? I mean, these are plenty."

Neil looked at his watch again, "We're all going to build the next project."

Anne said slowly, "Wait, are you talking about Little Tech Lab or the Big Tech Lab?"

Neil casually said, "Oh, I prefer Little Tech Lab where I modified the boards. But our next project will be in Big Tech Lab."

Yang looked amused, "Our project?"

Neil looked up, looked at his watch again, then smiled as he said, "Look up, it's right on time."

Flying in from the ocean, floating noiselessly about one hundred and fifty meters above them, seemingly covering the sky was one of the largest AeroLifters ever built, about the size of a small aircraft carrier.

Yang raised his palms upward and said, "Yeah, so. Three or four of those land at the air field every day."

Neil responded softly, "Let's go in for dinner and I'll explain our new project."

They caught one last wave, changed in the locker rooms, locked up their new boards, and headed upstairs for dinner. As promised, their table, in the corner by the window, was waiting. Neil ordered the ostrich burger, Yang and Anne bison burgers, and Ellie the wild boar burger. They waited until the waiter walked away out of ear-shot.

They all leaned in.

Anne said, "Sooo?"

Neil looked back at all of them, "Remember the research trip we went on after we won our first Science Quiz Bowl?"

Ellie was quick to respond, "Who could forget a balloon safari over Kenya to track elephant herd movement?"

Yang smiled, "I liked this year's prize, going to the Arctic to drill ice core samples."

Neil nodded in agreement, "But what was the one thing that went wrong on that first trip?"

Anne smiled and said, "Besides having the wind blow my favorite 2030 World Series hat off my head, out of the balloon basket, and into the path of fifty elephants?"

Yang rolled his eyes, "What could be worse?"

Neil gave her a sympathetic nod, "Well I was thinking more like when that wind blew, it changed direction and the balloon went in a different direction from the herd. We lost a day's worth of tracking data."

Ellie said pointedly, "Not much we could have done about that."

Neil nodded in agreement, "Nothing then, not the way regular air balloons are subject to the whims of air currents. But a new and improved version would be very helpful."

Yang looked hopeful, "I have a new idea for an electrical generator that would fit in the bottom of every shoe. Every time you walk or run, the pressure generates electricity, which is stored in a micro-battery. You then plug it into the grid at night. Times a billion people. It would have an impact."

Neil grimaced, "Sorry, some 16 year old just built one. It was announced last week in 'Energy Daily'."

Yang pursed his lips, "That's the trouble with being 18, all these youngsters are starting to eclipse us."

Ellie leaned forward, "OK, OK, tell us about your plan."

Neil reached into his pocket and pulled out his com-phone, pulled out a hair-thin wire from each side, pulled them side-ways, then up. The nano-carbon wires were thin but amazingly strong and they stayed upright. The wires formed a barely visible rectangle and within a second a large virtual screen appeared between the wires. Neil talked at the device, "Balloon Project Diagram on screen." The little device talked back, "Code required for this request." Neil leaned in and whispered, "Sci Team Project 17."

The others grinned.

Just as the illustration was appearing, their meal arrived. Neil quickly said, "Dim." The screen went dark.

The waiter passed out their plates and left.

Neil whispered, "Restart." The screen came back on.

Neil quietly said, "I was thinking something like this."

They all took big bites of their burgers and leaned in, blocking anyone else from seeing the screen.

Neil finished chewing and stated, "AeroLifters are massive and control their direction with huge propellers. But what we need is a smaller version for scientists, explorers, and researchers."

Ellie, still staring at the screen said, "This will revolutionize exploration. This will really help."

Yang, excited and taking another bite, blurted out, "Every kid in the world will want one. You'll be rich."

Anne's eyes got wide, "Rich like the guy who cured baldness?"

Ellie shook her head, "No one could be that rich."

Neil looked at his friends, "I didn't think of this to get rich. I just think it's kind of a good idea."

Yang looked at Ellie and Anne, then at Neil, "OK, We're in. What do we need to do?"

CHAPTER 8

Neil grinned and said, "Well, the most important thing we need to do is…" he leaned in, and the others leaned in closely also, "is to finish our meal."

Ellie threw a napkin at Neil.

Yang flagged down the server, "A round of mango ginger milkshakes for dessert please."

After they finished their burgers and shakes, Anne looked excited, "OK we're ready. Now what?"

Neil said, "Let's meet at the Tech Lab and I'll fill you in there. We need a van and Mr. Garcia is letting us use the Tech Lab's van."

Anne said, "This sounds like it's going to be big."

Ellie, taking the cue, said, "Remember what Mr. Garcia said…" Neil, Anne, and Ellie completed the sentence, "It's not how tall the Tech Lab ceiling is, it's how tall the Tech Lab doors are."

As they were getting up to leave, Yang, closed his eyes, and meekly said, "I know, I know. I wish he had mentioned that before I finished my last project."

They all walked out to the parking lot, mounted their Tryx and headed south along Ocean Avenue.

After a quick drive they ended up back at their old high school, where they wound through the parking lot to the back of the school. They pulled up to a tall building, taller than a typical gym facility, and parked. This time the license plates read: SciTeam1, SciTeam2, SciTeam4, SciTeam3. They got off their Tryx, and as Neil and Anne proceeded to the building to turn on the lights, Yang stopped and looked back. Quizzically he said, "Hey the numbers are out of order."

Ellie smiled and said, "I know. I was just seeing if you'd notice."

Yang said flatly, "It is bad luck for numbers to be out of order."

Ellie shot back quickly, "There is no such thing as luck."

Yang, shrugged and said, "There is, my grandmother says the numbers should always line up."

Ellie smiled again and said, "They should, and that's why you are so good at math."

She put her arm around his shoulders and said, "Now let's get inside with the others."

As they were walking in, Yang whispered, "There is."

Ellie whispered, "There isn't."

They entered the Tech Lab which was huge and looked more like an airport hangar. To the left of the door, in one corner, were some desks, chairs, computers, screens, and digital chalkboards facing away from the door. To the right of the door were other larger more industrial equipment such as pulleys, drill presses, lathes, belt saws, and a myriad of other tools. There were parts, scraps, and dust everywhere, testimony to the years of projects that countless students had created. The middle area had been cleared out by Neil and was wide open, ready for the start of Project 17. Ellie and Yang walked around a very large screen and could then see that Neil already had his diagram up again.

Neil pointed to the screen and said, "Switch to Component List." The screen showed a short list of materials and sizes.

He continued, "I already ordered and received the helium tanks, the rolls of Mylar for the bladder, the nano-Kevlar for the protective covering, and the solar film."

Anne asked, "How did you get all that?"

Neil responded, "Mr. Garcia said to put the materials on his account. A graduation present for our last project together. He just wanted a copy of the blueprints for his files, which I gladly gave him."

"But wait," piped in Ellie, "we still need a cabin, cords, fans…"

"I know," said Neil quickly, "I maxed out the account on the priority items. That's why Mr. Garcia lent us the van, so we could scrounge for the remaining parts. I'm just not sure where to get these final pieces."

Anne looked calmly at Neil, "Well if you didn't always order new perfect parts from Pete's Perfect Parts Depot you wouldn't run over budget."

Neil sputtered, "There's no such place as Pete's…"

Anne held up her hand, "All I'm saying, is that if you buy one-hundred percent perfect parts, you pay one hundred percent."

Yang, nodded at Neil empathetically, "That makes sense."

Anne continued, "It does if you have an unlimited budget. I propose we get the remaining parts that are maybe only ninety-nine percent perfect but free."

Yang raised his eyebrows at Neil, "Your point makes sense, hers makes more better sense."

Neil looked quizzical, "You've been out of school a week and you toss grammar out the window?"

"Grammar schmammar," said Yang quietly. "Don't worry about the grammar, I'm making a point."

"All right," said Neil, as he looked at the other three, "where do we go to get these ninety-nine percent parts?" Anne gave a big smile, "Road trip! Neil you drive, I'll give directions. Where's the van?"

"I parked it in the back of the lab," said Neil happily.

They all walked through the darkened lab to the back where an oversized van waited. They hopped in the cab, which was big enough for all four to sit up front. The massive rear doors of the lab rolled up, they departed, and the doors rolled down with a deep thud.

After winding through town, they headed east on Route 15 toward the Mojave Desert. It was now late evening and the desert, with no clouds in the sky, seemed illuminated by millions of stars. The van hummed along at a good clip while the four joked, talked, and sang to the music blaring from the stereo.

After about an hour's drive Ellie said, "We should be close. Look for a small sign that says RHZ #73."

Neil asked, "What's RHZ?"

"Recycling Holding Zone," responded Ellie.

Neil drove for another minute, then asked, "What's a Recycling Holding Zone?"

"Oh there's the sign," Ellie said excitedly and pointed to a plain white sign with green lettering 'RHZ #73'.

They turned and another sign read 'Drop Off' with an arrow to the left and 'Pick Up' with an arrow to the right. Not too far down the road they could see the glow of what looked like stadium lights. They steered right and followed a dusty road to the Pick Up area. They parked among dozens of other cars and trucks, then clambered out and walked into the two-story wooden office. Behind the long counter were three signs: the top one, in green lettering, read 'Recycling Holding Zone #73', beneath that, also in green lettering, 'Number of Liters of Oil Saved by Recycling', and the bottom sign, in electric green LED lights, showed numbers, into the billions. The numbers were constantly changing, always going up, and the last few numbers were changing so fast it was hard to read.

An elderly manager looked up from an e-reader, smiled, and said, "Welcome to RHZ 73, may I help you?"
Anne moved ahead of the others, "Mr. Truett?"
"Anne?" responded the manager with an even bigger smile. "My how you've grown."
"Mr. Truett," Anne said looking at him, then turning, "these are my friends Neil, Yang, and Ellie."
Each smiled and waved.
Mr. Truett walked out from behind the counter and greeted each one warmly, then said, "I've known Anne for years. Years ago, her father and I helped pass the laws making recycling mandatory. The country saved so much energy and created so many jobs it helped move the economy forward by a big leap. I've since retired, but work here periodically just for fun. I take the late shift so one of the younger managers can take an early shift."
Neil cleared his throat, "I thought recycling just meant melting everything back down to its original material. So what does this place do?"
"He needs to get out of the lab more," joked Ellie as she rubbed Neil's shoulder.

"I take it you've never had a tour here before?" said Truett to Neil.

Neil shook his head no.

"Let's go upstairs then and we'll show Neil here a little sight," said Truett as he led them to the stairs. They quickly climbed to the second floor which had offices on the front side and floor to ceiling windows on the back facing into the storage area. They looked out through the windows. The little sight was truly awe inspiring, an array of literally everything ever made, laid out for thousands of acres, glittering in the flood lights. Decas of people and forklifts scurried about.

Mr. Truett started in on his brief speech he'd made hundreds of times before. "Recycling does bring unused items down to their original materials. However, there are millions of items that are new or have been used for such a short period that they are essentially new. Items come from failed businesses, unclaimed items in warehouses or loading docks, unsold items from estate sales, etc. All these items have value for somebody. More value than melting them down. We hold them here in the relatively moisture-free desert. This place originally stored retired military planes, then civilian planes, then after recycling became mandatory, high quality items came here rather than going to the dump. And they are here for the asking. So they are free if you are starting a business and plan to help the economy. If you need motors, desks, lighting, or whatever, this is the place to come first."

Anne stood next to Mr. Truett and said, "Ninety nine percent perfect parts for free."

Mr. Truett looked at Anne and said, "Hey, I like your sales pitch better."

"We have boiled parts, fried parts, barbeque parts, parts stew, parts chowder, steamed parts…" continued Anne in her best Bubba Gump imitation.

Neil looked at Anne, smiled and shook his head while saying, "OK, OK, I get it."

He then turned to Mr. Truett and said, "I'm sold." He pulled out his com-phone, put it on the table, opened it up, then said, "Project 17, parts list." The list came on the screen. Neil stepped aside so Truett could see the screen and asked, "Can we get these items? The ones highlighted in yellow we have already acquired, the non-highlighted ones we still need to obtain."

Truett looked at the list, "Interesting list. I think we have all of these." He pulled out a small scanner from his pocket and asked Neil, "May I?"

"Of course," said Neil.

Truett scanned the list, turned to the window and said, "Screen on." The window instantly became a large screen with a box that stated 'Input List,' he pointed the scanner at the screen and clicked it. The list appeared on the screen and right away the screen became a grid with every item on the list sliding to a point on the grid.

"Yes, it looks like we have all the items on your list. Do you want them now?" asked Mr. Truett.

"Yes, please," said Ellie.

"We brought a good size truck," said Yang.

"Bring the truck around to the loading dock. Just follow the signs. The picking teams will pick the items and load them on your truck," said Truett. He continued, "It's pretty late. If you're hungry you can grab a bite at the café here while you wait. I recommend the avocado, black bean, and goat cheese burrito."

Down at the small but clean café, which was fairly full considering the time of day, they all chowed down on their burritos. Over the intercom came a pleasant voice saying, "Sunflower Enterprises, your parts are ready." A small group got up from a far table and made their way to the exit.

Ellie said, "These are delicious."

Yang, with a huge mouthful could only nod in agreement.

They sat quietly, full, and contented, until another blast from the intercom, "Project Seventeen, your parts are ready."

"That was fast," Yang commented.

"Well, we should be grateful. I can't wait to get started," said Anne.

A pause while they looked at each other. "Are we pulling an all-nighter?" asked Ellie. The others nodded enthusiastically. All four did a subtle fist bump and quietly said, "Sci Team." They each took one last big bite of their burritos finishing them off, got up, and headed for the pick-up area.

They loaded up and headed out to the highway. Too excited to sleep, they cranked some tunes while they discussed their tasks and took turns driving back to the lab.

CHAPTER 9

They backed the van into the Tech Lab, stopped to the now familiar sound of airbrakes, and then jumped out. Yang started up the fork-lift and hauled the items out of the van. Then the real work began: cutting, grinding, welding, and decas of other assembly steps. Sparks, dust, clanging, and scraps were everywhere. Every now and then a voice would rise above the din, "I need a hoist," and, "The Mylar speed bonder just jammed." After several hours the noise subsided as each subsection was completed. They connected all the subcomponents together, drifted over to the desk area, and sat down.

Neil finally said, "I think we're done."
"We're not done till we've had a test flight," said Anne.
"I agree," said Ellie.
"I'm up for a maiden voyage, I'm still wide awake, but starving." said Yang.
The others nodded, indicating they too were hungry.
"I'll go and pick up some breakfast, while you all go through the checklist," said Yang as he headed out.

Every project they had worked on together had a checklist. Anne and Ellie stood up and walked back over to the work area.
Neil talked into his com-phone, "Project 17. Checklist. No specs. Open."
On the screen was the list of parts but without all the specifications. "Let's do the outside first." Neil called them off and either Anne or Ellie responded.

"Mylar balloon filled with helium."
"Listening for leaks…..no leaks. Check."
"Protective nano-Kevlar covering."
"Looks taut. Check."
"Nano-carbon cables to hold the balloon."
"Connections holding. Check."
"Flexi-solar panels."
"Check."
"Connecting wires."
"Check."
 "Roof storage rack."
"All points look soldered. Check."
"Lithium-air batteries."
"Check."
"Lights."
"Lights in place. Check."
"Cabin."
"Check."
"Industrial Dyson fans."
"Check."
"Struts,"
"Check."
"Wheels and pontoons."
"Check."
"Great, let's check the inside."
Ellie and Anne climbed inside.
"Hey, it's got a small fridge."
"That's a bonus feature, not on the checklist. Fan directional controller."
"Fans swivel. Check."
 "Battery gauges."

"Gauges working. Batteries charged. Check."
"GPS"
"Check."
"Checklist complete. Thank you."

Anne and Ellie walked back to the desk area. They all looked back at their new contraption. "Looking good," admired Ellie.

"Needs one more thing," said Anne. She skipped back to the work area, opened a few storage lockers, "This should do it." Then they heard a faint hissing sound.

Neil looked quizzically at Ellie who just shrugged.

Yang arrived with breakfast, "If we're going to take it out we should go now. The sky is looking a little gray in the distance."

Anne walked back, "Let's go then."

Ellie said, "Let's have breakfast in the balloon. You all get in, I'll open the front door."

The three climbed in the cabin while Ellie opened the large front door, equally as large as the back entrance door. She then ran back to the cabin as the fans started and began kicking up dust.

The airship, newly named 'SS Sci Team' with a can of spray paint, slowly nosed out of the open doors. The balloon cleared the door and hovered slowly in the parking lot.

Neil, barely able to hide his enthusiasm, said, "Wow, it really works!"

Yang, also enthusiastic, said, "Let it rip, Captain."

Neil worked the joy stick, and the airship slowly rose and went forward.

A couple of people out jogging stopped and stared. A car came to a stop as the driver leaned out of the window to get a better look. A girl rollerblading in a bikini, stopped and waved. It was by far the coolest sight anyone had seen.

The SS Sci Team continued to slowly rise, did a test circle above the school, then took off at a steady climb heading west to the beach. They were oblivious of the storm to the north.

CHAPTER 10

Anne was giddy, "This is great."

Ellie added, "What a view."

Yang pointed and said, "Look there's the park."

Anne's eyes lit up, "Let's head to the beach and see who's surfing."

Yang nodded, "Yeah, let's buzz Bill's."

Neil, said happily, "All right, I think I can get us there."

Ellie quickly said, "Do we need to program the GPS?"

Neil pointed, "No, I can see the ocean from here."

They all looked forward.

"I've been looking down this whole time, I hadn't even noticed we were up high enough to see that far," said Ellie.

Yang went to the fridge and got out the grapefruit juice jugs and passed them around. He cleared his throat, "I think Neil was right, every scientist will want one of these, and every sight-seeing company, and every search and rescue, and just about everyone. Here's to Neil."

They all hoisted their juice jugs. Yang, Ellie, and Anne all said, "Cheers!" They took a sip.

"And here's to you all, the best Sci Team in the business," replied Neil.

They said cheers again and took another sip.

Anne was smiling, "Now we are way more than a science team….we have our own airship…this could be a business!"

Ellie, Yang, Anne, and Neil all lifted their juice jugs again, "Cheers!" and took a final gulp.

Ellie looked out the front, "We're at the ocean." They all turned and looked out.

Anne commented, "I see some dolphins, let's see if we can keep up with them."

Neil took the SS Sci Team down a bit as he steered to follow the dolphins. It was a beautiful sight being directly above a pod racing with the waves.

Ellie commented, "We don't seem to be bothering them at all."

Everyone was looking down at the dolphins when all of a sudden the sky got very dark. They immediately looked up. An AeroLifter was coming in for a landing and was directly overhead. Neil steered their airship south for a few seconds and then back up slightly to be even with their much, much larger cousin. The Captain of the AeroLifter waved. The Sci Team waved back.

The AeroLifter passed and they looked back down to the dolphins which by now had moved on.

Yang said, "Let's head north towards Bill's."

Everyone nodded. They followed the coastline and quickly were above the surfers out for the morning waves. They steered down slightly and watched the surfers up close. Some of the surfers sitting on their boards started pointing northward frantically, and all of them quickly caught the next wave and headed in.

"It looks like the surfers are heading in," said Ellie.

Anne squinted and looked out at the waves intently, "Yeah, the waves look a little choppy." She looked up, "Hey look north. There's a reason the waves are choppy." Everyone looked up.

"Looks like rain," said Neil.

"It looks like a monsoon," said Ellie.

"It's getting dark, too. That is a huge storm," said Anne.

"Well that came in much faster than I thought an hour ago," said Yang.

Ellie sounded worried, "Maybe we should turn back."

Neil, sounding steady, said, "You're right, safety first, we can finish our test run later." Neil steered back toward land.

Ellie looked concerned, "The storm's getting bigger. We're not making much headway."

Yang quickly stated, "Can't we follow the AeroLifter?"

Neil, not sounding as steady, said, "I think the airfield is too far away, this storm is coming really fast."

"Can we get above the storm?" asked Anne.

Neil looked directly at Anne, and sounding grateful said, "Good idea, let's try that." Neil commenced a steady climb.

Ellie, sounding a bit relieved, said, "It's a little calmer up here. But we're still not getting anywhere."

Anne looked at Neil, and slid her arm through his, "Try higher."

Ellie looked down, "I can't see the ground at all, anywhere. It looks like one of those trans-regional storms."

The airship was getting buffeted pretty hard. Neil stated flatly, "Not only are we not making headway, but we are getting blown way off course."

Yang asked quietly, "Did anyone bring an oxygen mask?

Neil responded quietly also, "We didn't pack any emergency supplies. We were just going for a test run."

Anne said somberly, "A three hour tour."

Ellie looked at Anne, "Don't joke, this is getting scary."

The dark clouds, wind, and lightning were getting worse. The Sci Team airship was now getting buffeted severely.

Neil tried to sound reassuring, "Nothing's going to go wrong. Just hold on."

Anne looked at Ellie, and, hugging her tightly, said, "I think we're going to be late for lunch."

A huge gust of wind sent the airship soaring upward. Then, everything went black.

CHAPTER 11

Everything was black in the jungle except for six flashlight beams that darted around. Then one beam shone upwards. "Over here," a raspy voice said. The other beams quickly converged on the voice. "Look up," said the voice. All the beams shone upwards to discover a shiny silver cabin, which dangled from the trees.

"Climb up and see if anyone is there," said a deep calm voice.

Immediately there was rustling of branches and leaves. Then, from inside the cabin came the raspy voice, "Four." The calm voice said, "Bring them down please…and be gentle." The calm voice continued into his phone, "We'll need a Jungle Trekker at my location, straight away, please."

A few minutes later, the Jungle Trekker, a dark green, long wheelbase, four-wheel drive vehicle with wide knobby tires, arrived. The four new arrivees, barely breathing, were loaded into the passenger compartment and the Jungle Trekker headed back. It was followed by the six Mini Jungle Trekkers, Segway-like vehicles but with tank treads instead of tires.

CHAPTER 12

Yang was the first to wake. He narrowly opened his eyes, looked up for a moment then looked down his nose. He reached up gingerly and pulled off an oxygen tube in his nose. His eyes widened as he looked sideways and saw the others, also in cots with oxygen tubes. He sat up and whispered, "Neil…Neil. Are you awake?

Anne sat up, "I'm awake…what's this?" She pulled the oxygen tube out. "Ellie wake up….Yang where are we?"

Yang looked at Anne, "I don't know."

Neil woke up. He opened his eyes, sat up, looked at the others, and said, "Are you OK?"

Anne nodded, Yang nodded.

Anne repeated, "Ellie wake up."

Yang got up and looked out of the window, or rather hundreds of windows that formed a huge dome. "Neil, Anne, you have to see this."

Neil and Anne got up and looked out of the windows. They were slightly above canopy level and could see nothing but jungle for kilometers.

"Well…we're not in California anymore," whispered Anne.

Neil looked at Anne and said, "Is this what you meant by getting out of the lab more often?"

Anne grinned and walked back to Ellie's cot. She gently stroked Ellie's forehead, and at her touch Ellie woke up. "Ohhhhhh," murmured Ellie.

Neil and Yang turned and came back to Ellie's cot.

Anne, looking concerned asked, "Where does it hurt?"

"Doesn't hurt…just very woozy," replied Ellie.

"Try this," said a silky voice, as a beautiful young black woman entered the room carrying a tray with four cups. She walked over to Ellie first, placed the tray on a nearby desk and handed the cups out. They all stared wide-eyed as they took the cups and took sips.

"Thank you," said Yang as he elbowed in front of Neil. The others followed suit, lifted their cups, and said thanks.

"This is delicious," said Ellie, "I'm feeling better already."

"It's a local brew," said the young woman with a smile.

"Speaking of local," Neil raised his cup again as if to make a point with it, "where are we?"

Anne stepped forward, "Perhaps we should introduce ourselves before we ask our kind host questions."

Neil raised his eyebrows, "Sorry, I didn't mean to be rude."

"Not at all," said the same calm voice from the jungle as a tall handsome black man with short gray hair and a short gray beard walked into the room. "My daughter's name is Mae, and my name is Wally. You are in my lab in Brazil."

Anne shook their hands, "Thank you for your hospitality, I'm …"

"Anne," interjected Wally. He shook each of their hands and called them each by name. He continued, "When my assistants brought you in from your airship, you were unconscious. We scanned you for any internal damage, which I'm happy to report showed nothing but healthy bones and organs. You were out for some time but I think you will have no long-term effects."

"The last thing I remember was going fairly high up," said Ellie.

"I think your airship must have been caught in the derecho that hit the west coast of the U.S. It lifted you high enough to lose oxygen, where you passed out from hypoxia, and were then carried by the jet stream down here. Luckily you weren't at that high altitude long enough to cause any damage. There's precedent for this. In 1959, a military pilot had to bail out over a cumulonimbus cloud and bounced around inside the storm for thirty minutes before he landed safely."

"This may have gone past a derecho and been an ARk storm," said Mae.

"I thought ARk storms were just hypothetical," said Ellie.

"The U.S. Weather Service has been warning about them for years. This storm went way beyond multiple derechos. I gather it hit the levels of an ARk storm, but all the data isn't in yet." responded Wally.

"Well, at least we got a good night's sleep," laughed Anne.

"Speak for yourself. That was an awful storm. I never want to go through that again," said Ellie flatly.

"Um…how do you know our names? And how did you know we came from the U.S.?" asked a bewildered Yang.

"We also scanned your fingerprints," smiled Wally. "I am also happy to report that you have straight As, no criminal record, and no over-due library books."

They all beamed.

"However, there was one speeding ticket."

Yang, Ellie, and Anne all looked at Neil.

"I made a few adjustments to our Tryx and was just doing a road test," said Neil sheepishly.

"321 kilometers per hour is some adjustment," said Wally with a proud smile.

Anne gave Neil a subtle low five.

"We should call our parents," said Ellie.

"And work," said Yang.

"Already been done," said Mae, "We forwarded your info to the White House and they made the calls."

"Thank you," said Anne.

Neil raised his hand slightly, as if he was still in class, "You're not really Wally…You're Dr. Walstib aren't you?"

CHAPTER 13

Ellie whispered, "Neil, what are you talking about? Dr. Walstib is an urban myth, a persona to front for the Walstib Corporation."

"The rest of the world does know me as Dr. Walstib," began Wally. "However to my family, friends, colleagues, and," he gestured to the four, "to four explorers extraordinaire, I am simply Wally."

Yang, looked intrigued, "Do you really have more patents than anyone in the world?"

Wally looked embarrassed, "Yes, but some I share with my daughter."

Mae, standing behind Dr. Walstib, winced, shook her head, and held up eight fingers.

Anne, looked stunned, "But you're famous. How come we've never seen a picture of you?"

"I don't need to be famous. I need for my work to help people," said Dr. Walstib earnestly.

Mae affectionately took her father by the arm, "He's not really part of the club scene."

Dr. Walstib turned to Neil, "Did you just build your airship? I could smell the Mylar bonding."

Neil looked at his three friends, "We all did."

"Do you consider the speeding ticket and the crash landing to be failures?" Walstib said as he continued to look directly at Neil.

"I suppose so," Neil said slowly.

Walstib put his arms around all of them, "I don't. I've had ten times more failures than patents. Each failure was just a step on the path. It's part of the process. My solar panels

took decas, if not hundreds, of mistakes before the final
product came together. You know the famous lubricant
WD-40?"
They all nodded.
"So named as the first thirty-nine formulas failed. I'll buy
one of those airships of yours, if you'll make me one."
The four nodded enthusiastically and looked at each other.
"Why so secretive? Why did you check us out so
thoroughly?" inquired Anne.
Walstib looked out the window, "A lot of people want to
know where I am. Industrial espionage – stealing trade
secrets, stealing research methodology, etc. – is big
business. I have relocated much of my research here in the
middle of the rain forest to be as far from prying eyes as
possible. I checked you all out because there are those who
don't find their way here by accident. They get escorted out
rather briskly."
Neil said quietly, "We were taking our airship out for a
very brief initial test flight and I never thought to check the
weather."
"Always check the weather," said Walstib with a smile.
"Yes, Sir," replied Neil.
"Call me Wally," said Walstib. "Besides, have you seen
that forecaster on the Weather Channel? She is so…."
"Dad!" cut in Mae.

CHAPTER 14

Mae started to collect the tea cups, "I'll get you set up in our guest quarters, as it looks like you'll be here a little longer."

"Thank you," said Neil as he handed her his cup. "How bad is the airship?"

"Your airship is being taken out of the trees by our assistants and then we'll see about repairs," replied Mae.

"So just relax, not much happens around here," said Walstib.

Mae, as she was about to carry off the cups turned back to the four friends and mouthed, "Nothing."

Just then a loud warning buzzer went off.

Walstib spun around and ran to a video screen that took up an entire interior wall. Mae and the Sci Team followed.

"Location please," he said quickly. A large map appeared with a concentric circle grid overlay. A red line outlined one particular sector. "Sector D-1," said a soothing female computer voice.

"Sat visual please," Walstib continued.

"Satellite locking in," said the soothing voice. The grid image gave way to a bird's eye view, smoke was visible.

"Ground visual please," Walstib sounded slightly less calm. The large satellite visual faded to six smaller images from six ground based cameras. It was quickly obvious where the problem was.

"Expand camera D-1-6 please."

The other screens faded and sector D-1-6 expanded to fill the entire wall. The sector, a rugged mountainous looking area, was filled with smoke.

"Fire on the mountain…not good," said Walstib crisply. As soon as he said that the screen showed multiple sets of legs running around the area. "Poachers…even worse. I'm going to need some help," he said looking at his four new house guests.

Neil looked at the others who all nodded, "Happy to help. What can we do?"

"Follow me," said Walstib as he started sprinting down the hall. "Elevator open," he barked, "please," he added.

Mae and her four new friends followed down the hall quickly. They reached a large industrial size elevator and piled in.

"Garage level, please," stated Walstib. As they were going down, Walstib commented, "You're lucky you landed in sector E-4, a much more hospitable area, D-1 is rather difficult."

Ellie, trying to be helpful, asked, "Will your assistants help too?"

Walstib looked at Mae, who answered, "They get a little skittish around fire."

The Sci Team tried to hide their quizzical looks to each other.

The doors opened to a huge underground garage with a long row of neatly parked cars, trucks, and Jungle Trekkers.

"This way," said Walstib as he walked quickly down the row. Toward the end of the row were eight vehicles the Sci Team had never seen before – low slung, metallic-glass, egg-shaped cars with retractable tubular struts connected to wide knobby tires. And each car had a row of launch tubes attached to the rear of the vehicle.

"Capture Trekkers one through six, open," commanded Walstib, and the first six canopies hinged upward like the canopy of a jet plane. "Climb in. I'll take lead, Mae will take the rear, everyone else take the middle. Everything is voice-activated. Your gauges and capture options are on a heads-up display projected on the canopy. I'll fill you in once we get going."

They all slid in, the seats were like race car seats, snug, designed to keep the occupants stable during a bumpy ride.

"This looks ominous," said Ellie under her breath.

"I heard that," Ellie heard Walstib say through the car speakers. Walstib continued, "We are all connected electronically. Garage doors 34 through 39 open. Let's move out."

The six garage doors opened. The drivers pushed their green start buttons and inched forward through the doors. Walstib raced forward with Neil, Anne, Ellie, Yang, and Mae in quick succession. The heavy garage doors closed with a thud behind them.

CHAPTER 15

The Capture Trekkers were fast, agile, and quiet. They were also clear, designed to be very hard to see from any vantage point, from the jungle canopy or from the side. The vehicles raced through the jungle following the lead car, single file. When the cars went through a narrow opening, such as between two trees that were close together, the servo motors retracted the tubular struts. And after the onboard camera saw that the Trekker was clear of the obstruction the struts were pushed back out again for stability.

Wally obviously knows his way around this jungle, he mustn't spend all his time in the lab, thought Yang to himself. He wondered if Wally walked the jungle for meditation or to think through vexing problems. Both he concluded.
"Normally we use these cars to chase down animals for research purposes or to catch one that is wounded so we can nurse it back to health," Wally's voice signaled to each car. "However, occasionally we also need to catch poachers, like this group. Don't worry, the Capture Trekkers are made of bullet-proof metallic-glass."
Anne raised her eyebrows and mouthed, "Bullet-proof?"
Neil just smiled and mouthed, "Cool."
"We are getting close, I see smoke up ahead," said Walstib. "Once they see us they'll split up and try to make a run for it. I'll go for the first one to break and you all just follow the closest ones to you. Use the large net option for groups of two or more, use the small net option for individuals.

Use your voice to say the option, then say fire, and the launcher will target the closest poacher."

CHAPTER 16

The Capture Trekkers continued to make their way forward unnoticed. In what should have been a healthy, pristine, and quiet rain forest setting, it looked quite the opposite. There were ten or so rough looking, hired hands, some with torches, some with butterfly nets, and some with glass jars. There was fire, smoke, and loud shouting. The men with the torches were waving them in the trees and bushes, while others with nets collected huge spiders as they leaped away from the flames. The other men took the spiders from the nets, transferred them into the glass jars, and put the jars into racks in the back of several new black Land Rovers. The sides of the Rovers had the logo AUCO.

The cavalry arrived in the form of six stealthy Capture Trekkers, now with headlights on to better see in the low light at ground level. The poachers panicked and ran in every direction. Walstib peeled off right after the first one and gave chase. Two men stopped in bewilderment and Neil came up fast from behind the peeling off Walstib and surprised them. He drove straight at them, then came to a stop as they huddle, like deer caught in the headlights. "Large Net – Fire," shouted Neil. In-car cameras spotted the men, displayed their images on the windshield and one of the rear-mounted launchers let off a blast. A red ring was displayed on the windshield, the windshield beeped as the red ring enveloped the images on the windshield. Neil looked out at the two poachers and sure enough, they were enveloped by the net.

Anne veered to follow two men sprinting away to the left. She floored the accelerator pedal and gave chase. As she bore down on them she commanded, "Large Net – Fire." The images appeared on her windshield, but at the sound of the launcher the men split up. The net captured one but missed the other. "Ahhhh," Anne shouted, as she slammed on the brakes, turned and floored it again to give chase to the missed poacher. The running men were no match for the Trekkers and Anne quickly caught up to make her second capture. "Best game ever!" she whispered.

Ellie followed three men all running together as they aimed for rocky terrain. They were running fast but stopped abruptly as they came upon a small cliff. They turned around just in time to see a large net wrap tightly around them.

Yang followed one who had obviously played football as he zigged and zagged through the trees. He sensed a pattern and headed straight through the middle and fired just as the poacher crossed again, back over the middle path.

Mae had been following one who kept running in circles, hiding behind trees so that she raced right past him. Cleverly engineered, the Trekkers could spin 180 degrees in place and Mae got closer and closer each time the poacher momentarily stopped. For a mere second he bent over to catch his breath and Mae went in for the capture.

Walstib's target got the early jump and had a lead. After a lot of maneuvering the poacher seemed to disappear, but Walstib saw him drop to the ground. He circled around and then, out of the corner of his eye, saw feet sticking out of the end of a huge hollow log. Walstib flicked a switch that

turned on his outside speakers and said, "Do you know
what jungle creatures live in hollowed-out logs?"
The poacher paused for a moment, as if letting this question
sink in, then wriggled backward rapidly to get out of the
log. As soon as he stood up he felt the smooth hemp netting
wrapped around his body.

Walstib called to the others, "Wally here. I've got one.
How's everyone else doing?"
"This is Mae, I've got one."
"This is Yang, I've got one."
"Anne here, I got two."
"Ellie here, do I get a plaque? I got three."
"Neil, checking in, I got two."
Walstib sounded pleased, "All right. Let's circle back to the
original point of engagement." They all circled back to the
Poachers' trucks and climbed out of their Trekkers.

Mae was the first to see her, she pointed and yelled, "Dad!
Look!"
Not far from the parked Rovers was a woman tied to a tree
struggling to get loose. She was in her forties, an attractive
outdoorsy type, dressed in blue jeans and a tie-dye t-shirt
with dancing bears that read United Rainforest Coalition
International.
Walstib jumped out of his Trekker and ran up to her, untied
her, and asked quickly, "Althea, are you all right?"
Althea, still out of breath, "Yes…yes, I think so."
"What happened?"
"I was doing my rounds, weighing and recording the
amount of fruit peel and seeds that have been dropped at

certain trees to see if the monkey family still eats in the same location. You know, to check for any seasonal territorial patterns."

Walstib stared at her intently.

"Oh. These trucks came roaring by, they saw that I saw them, and they just grabbed me and took my com-phone."

"Do you know why they are doing this?" inquired Walstib.

"It appears they're collecting Theraphasa Blondi spiders, Brazil's largest spider. I haven't any idea what for. Several of us from URCI have heard reports of this going on around the entire rainforest."

"How many men did you see?" asked Walstib quickly.

Althea thought for a moment as she was standing up, then said, "I think twelve."

"We captured ten," he said as he looked at the others, now gathered around. "Let's poke around here, someone may be hiding."

As soon as Walstib said that, one of the poachers, who had been hiding, grabbed two of the dropped torches from the clearing, threw them into the jungle, jumped into a Land Rover, and started to drive off. Walstib reached into his cargo pants pocket, pulled out what looked like a small black flashlight. He aimed the device at the fleeing truck and pushed a button. A small dart fired out, struck the truck, and sent blue electric arcs flying. The truck rolled to a halt.

Walstib was angry. He ran over to the truck, grabbed the driver by the arm, and pulled him back to the others. "How many others escaped?"

No answer.

"Why are you here?"

No answer.

Walstib was about to ask another question when flames leapt up from where the torches had been tossed. Everyone started kicking dirt on the flames but the flames started growing.

Walstib kept a firm grip on the poacher as he pulled out his com-phone and commanded, "Contact Lab…Fire Bots." He moved the com-phone away from his mouth and looked at Mae, "How many do you think?"

Mae looked at the flames and held up ten fingers.

Walstib nodded and went back to the com-phone, "Ten. My coordinates. Immediate release." He put the com-phone away and spoke to everyone, "The Fire Bots will be here in a minute, don't get burned trying to put out the flames, let's just move the Trekkers and the trucks out of the way."

Walstib held onto the poacher tightly while everyone else hurried and moved the vehicles a good thirty to forty meters from the flames.

Once the vehicles had been moved a safe distance, Walstib again picked up his com-phone, "External call. Governor's office." He waited. Everyone's eyebrows went up a tick. Then, "Hello Governor. ….I'm fine thanks, bit of a hurry though. We've caught some poachers and hope you can send some troops to pick them up. …..Great, thank you. …..Yes, at my coordinates.. …Bye."

"Sir?" Ellie pointed to the flames.

Walstib looked at the flames, "Not to worry. It's sad that this much has burned. It won't spread quickly though with

yesterday's rain. The Fire Bots will be here in a second."
And just as he had finished talking a slight whirring could
be heard overhead. A fleet of ten un-manned Fire Bots,
each the size of a large honey dew melon, with a directional
jet nozzle at each corner, flew by and went straight at the
flames.

"Thermographic lenses to sense heat?" asked Neil.

"Yes," said Walstib. "And a regular lens to navigate."
A door slid open and nozzles jetted out fire retardant gel
which adhered to the brush and trees and expanded once it
hit the air. They went in order, the first five subdued the
flames and the remaining bots circled shooting at hot spots.
Once they sensed no additional heat, they flew off.

"Wow!" exclaimed Anne.

"Those are so cool!" added Yang.

"We hope they'll catch on," added Walstib, "faster and
cheaper than a fire truck."

They could hear the trucks before they could see them. But
in a minute four large military trucks rolled up and came to
a halt. The senior officer jumped out of the passenger seat
on the first truck and came over to Walstib. They shook
hands, "Hello Dr. Walstib."

"Hello Captain, thanks for coming."

"Always happy to take out the trash."

"We have eleven, we think one got away," said Walstib
with a hint of sadness.

"Well, it's getting dark," said the Captain. "Jaguars, Pumas,
and Ocelots all hunt at night. He'll wish he'd been
captured."

"Speaking of night," Walstib pulled out his com-phone. He spoke into it, "Capture nets. Lights. Now." He looked again at the Captain, "The capture nets have LED lights built in, you should have no trouble finding your poachers. Could you please give our friend Althea a ride back into town?"

"No trouble at all," replied the Captain.

"Captain, I'll release the spiders before we head out. And Wally, thanks," said Althea as she leaned in and gave Walstib a kiss on the cheek.

CHAPTER 17

They returned to the lab complex. "Garage doors. Thirty four through thirty nine. Open. Please." said Walstib, and the doors opened. Walstib, Mae, Neil, Anne, Ellie, and Yang drove their Capture Trekkers into the garage and parked. They climbed out and Walstib continued, "Leave them here, my assistants will clean them up." They went back up the elevator to the main floor.

As soon as they arrived at the top floor, a soft buzzer sounded and the soft female voice stated, "President Filho is calling."

Walstib immediately responded, "Answer. Screen." The large screen flicked on and showed a prominent looking man in his late sixties wearing a suit, standing behind his desk. He looked worried. Walstib spoke, "Hello, Mr. President, good to hear from you."

"Perhaps not, Dr. Walstib, I need your help."

"What can I do Sir?"

"Governor Cardoso tells me you had a fire incident in your territory."

"Yes, we did."

"There has been fire and heavy smoke detected in other territories. These incidents just start up, then die out just as mysteriously. Luckily, no one has been hurt. We don't know what to make of it. We have some evidence and some surveillance video. Could you please come take a look and help us out?"

"Of course, I'll come right away, but I should bring my new friends as well, they helped in capturing the poachers who caused the fire out here." As he spoke, he turned to the four to seek their approval. Thumbs up and nods all around. "That will be fine. Call me when you arrive. Thank you for coming so quickly," at that the President pushed a button on his desk and the screen went blank.

Ellie looked at the others, then at Walstib, "I think we need to clean up first if we're going to meet the President of Brazil."
"Good point. Let's get cleaned up. Mae, I believe you were going to show our guests to their rooms."
"Yes," said Mae, "right this way." They followed her as she lead them down the hall to the other end of the building. "You each have your own room," she continued, "with a shower and a waterless clothes washer. Your clothes will be ready before you finish your showers. See you back at the observation room in five minutes."

They were all back at the observation room in four and a half minutes. Freshly scrubbed.
"That was refreshing, thank you," effused Anne.
The others nodded and smiled.
"Glad you are with us to help," said Walstib, "right this way to the launch pad."

CHAPTER 18

Walstib spoke into his com-phone again, "Shuttle bus. Hangar canopy. Open." They heard a rumbling noise. "Right this way," offered Mae as she gestured to follow her. They went to the left side of the observation floor, exited a glass door, and entered a glass elevator. As the elevator went down, they stared in amazement as the canopy opening was still in progress. Row by row, hundreds of trees were tipping over, but they were tipping over in a very mechanized fashion. Once a space about sixty meters by thirty meters had tipped over, the base, what they thought had been the ground, lowered about three meters then slid back under the adjacent trees.

"I thought those were trees," said Yang, stunned. Walstib explained, "Those are solar panels made to look like trees. A band of them about a hundred meters wide encircles the lab. We mimic mostly palm trees and banana trees which have large fronds in order to receive the most light. We are totally self-sufficient here. Also, the trees act as a cover for everything underground so it won't be visible from above. Got that idea from Disney World. They have hundreds of miles of storage and tunnels under the park."

The glass elevator stopped and opened about three stories below ground level.
As they walked Anne asked, "But what about the original real trees?"
"We replanted them in areas that needed soil conservation."

After walking about twenty meters they arrived at the
Shuttle Bus, a smaller version of the old Space Shuttle. The
Shuttle Bus fuselage was black and the canopy, which ran
the length of the Shuttle Bus, was made out of the same
metallic glass as the Capture Trekkers. This glass, however,
had a red-gold tint from the gold infused into the canopy to
help reflect the infrared light. There were canards up front
with two jet nozzles inside each and delta wings in the back
with two jet nozzles in each. The eight wing-jets were for
upward thrust and maneuverability, with six small jets
grouped together in the back for forward thrust.

The entrance ladder was already extended and they
bounded up. Walstib sat in the pilot's seat with Mae beside
him in the navigator's seat. There were four rows of
passenger seats, two seats per row with a center aisle. The
Sci Team sat in the first two rows.
Walstib, flicked some switches and said, "Please buckle up.
Buckling up is the most important item on the pre-flight
checklist."
As Walstib admonished everyone to wear their seatbelts
Mae was mouthing the words she had heard too often.
Walstib flicked one more switch and the wing jets roared
on, although much quieter than a regular jet. The Shuttle
Bus lifted off. After clearing the height of the lab Walstib
steered south- east and squeezed the trigger on the joystick.
The rear jets kicked on and everyone could feel the g-forces
as they were pressed back into their seats. It was a much
faster take-off than a standard jet and achieved Mach 2
quickly.

Walstib, looked at Mae, "Now, shall I tell our new friends what happened the last time you didn't wear your seat belt?"

"Not my fault. I didn't know you were going to pull an evasive maneuver," retorted Mae.

Anne looked at Neil and mouthed, "Evasive maneuver?" Four seatbelt clicks could be heard.

"That's my point," chided Walstib, "one never knows."

Ellie, sensing a little tension, quickly asked, "How fast are we going?"

"How about if I say we're a little over 320 kilometers from Brasilia and it will take us seven minutes?" quizzed Walstib.

"Bzzz," said Yang, pretended he was hitting the buzzer at a science quiz. "Approximately 2500 kilometers per hour, Mach 2," he grinned.

"Does the sonic boom do any damage to the animals in the rain forest?" asked Neil.

"Computer controlled nano-motors oscillate the trailing edge of the wings and tail a thousand times a second. Just a tenth of a millimeter, enough to distort the airflow, precluding a sonic boom, but not enough to alter stability or directional control," responded Walstib.

"That was the option we didn't order on the SS Sci Team," smiled Anne.

CHAPTER 19

Seven minutes after takeoff, they arrived in Brasilia, the capital of Brazil, and set down on a helicopter landing pad outside the National Congress Building. The buildings looked as modern and impressive today as they did when they were completed in 1960.

As they unbuckled, Walstib turned and said, "Thank you for flying Wally's Shuttle Bus Service." Mae rolls her eyes, "Dad."

"What?"

As they climbed down the ladder Ellie spoke softly to Mae, "This shuttle is pretty cool. I think he's just proud."

Mae looked at her dad with a partial smile, "I think he thinks he's funny. I also think he needs to get out more."

"At least I didn't make a joke about no food on the flight." As soon as Walstib said that, he caught a certain hungry look on the Sci Team's faces.

They walked quickly up the stairs to the National Congress Building and entered the main door.

They were greeted by a formal looking man in his early thirties. He wore an impeccable suit with a tie the same color green as the Brazilian flag. They shook hands.

"Greetings Dr. Walstib, and to you Mae. I am Dr. Pontes, the President's Environmental Advisor."

Walstib introduced the Sci Team.

Pontes continued, "No need to call him, we saw you arrive. He will be ready to receive you in about fifteen minutes, he is finishing a previously scheduled meeting."

"Perfect. Hopefully, we can get to a cafeteria or someplace to grab a quick bite to eat. I have belatedly noticed that my friends here haven't eaten in some time."

"You are in luck." Dr. Pontes walked over to several large doors and gently opened one. They quietly walked into the back of a large conference hall. As they walked in, they heard the sounds of a conference, with hundreds of attendees, in progress. Dr. Pontes whispered, "Here are the snack tables. Take anything you need. Don't worry, this is my conference. I'll wait outside. Enjoy."

As it turned out Walstib and Mae were hungry too, and all six feasted on whole wheat bagels, fresh figs, and freshly squeezed orange juice. All excellent examples of the massive Brazilian agricultural sector thought Walstib.

"Oh my goodness, this stuff tastes great," said Anne.

The others could only nod in agreement as they consumed the fist-size figs.

Coming from the front of the conference hall, they could hear what sounded like a host at a podium, introducing the next speaker. The conference host had a rather droning voice, and every time he turned his head left and right to look at the audience, his lips moved away from the microphone, thus, they only caught snippets of his introduction: "As you all know, our next speaker has traveled……. the world…and visited ….several times... In addition…just finished her latest book on the…. and exposing of large scale… with the … and the energy construction projects with a …. to wildlife habitat destruction. She has been working on… and an in-depth,

ground-breaking analysis of scenarios that …
and…involving the studies of previous non-
governmental…and…agencies and other stakeholders in
their efforts…"

Walstib leaned in and whispered to the others, "I'd hate to
embarrass myself by falling asleep standing up. Let's head
back into the entrance hall."
As they quickly but gracefully exited the lecture hall, Neil
whispered to Anne, "I was about to say that."
Once they were in the entrance hall but before Dr. Pontes
spotted them, Yang quietly spoke, "I thought our Student
Council meetings were boring."
"Sorry to disillusion you," responded Walstib, "but as you
get older, the meetings get worse…or your tolerance
diminishes, I'm not sure which."

Pontes waved to them and they followed him to the
elevator. In the elevator, Dr. Pontes said, "What I will show
you I could easily have sent to your com-system. President
Filho, however, prefers face-to-face meetings." They got
out on the top floor, and went into the President's office as
a small group of business people were leaving.
"Enter! Enter! Do come in," said a gracious President
Filho. Dr. Pontes introduced the Sci Team to the President
who came from behind his desk to shake everyone's hand.
The Sci Team looked very pleased with themselves.
"Thanks for coming. Dr. Pontes will show you what we
have found so far."
A large screen on the side of the room blinked on. Pontes
aimed a remote at the screen and a large map of Brazil

came to view. "Here are the areas of known smoke sightings," as he clicked his pointer again, twelve red dots scattered throughout the country were superimposed on the map. "One of our Rangers down in the southern territories saw a truck with the letters 'AUCO' on the side. Once they saw him they took off. He yelled after them but they didn't stop. His concern primarily was to look at the area to make sure there were no hot spots from their torches that could flare up into a fire. He found this." Pontes held up a glass jar with one spider, "It's a Theraphasa Blondi. That's it. That's all we've got. A truck, twelve smoke sightings, and a spider."

"And unfortunately, I have yet another meeting," said the President. "I," he gestured at Pontes, "we, hope you can figure this out. You've been such a help in the past. So far this seems somewhat minor, but it's the sort of thing that might escalate and do some real damage to our precious rain forest." He paused, and added, visibly saddened, "We have lost too much of it in the past."
They all shook hands with the President as he bid them farewell.

Dr. Pontes escorted them to the elevator, "Please call if there is anything we can do to help. I hope this is merely a troublesome prank."

CHAPTER 20

They re-entered the Shuttle Bus and all made a good-natured point of buckling up. As soon as the jets kicked in, Mae said, "I think Althea thinks this was no prank." Walstib turned slightly and said, "Governments tend to downplay things until they become too obvious. Perhaps Pontes was just trying out a sound bite. What does anyone know about these spiders?" He turned north-west and squeezed the throttle.

Yang commented, "There are over 40,000 species of spiders. Everyone now realizes the value of the rainforest so I wonder what could be so worthwhile about this one species that it would be worth burning parts of the rainforest down just to get them."

"Fried spiders are a delicacy in Indonesia and a few other countries," offered Ellie.

Everyone grimaced and Mae said, "The demand can't be that great."

"Most spider bites are mild enough that they don't need any manufactured anti-venom. I wouldn't think anyone would need this large a quantity of spider venom," offered Anne.

"It can't be the silk, the new nano-silk is stronger," stated Neil.

"Stronger but still not as elastic," corrected Walstib.

"So someone is going to the not insignificant trouble of rounding up thousands of spiders. And, Althea said these are the biggest spiders in Brazil. What could you do with that much elastic spider silk?" asked Neil.

"Extreme trampoline?" offered Anne.

"Shuttle bus. Hangar canopy. Open please." Walstib said into the Shuttle Bus com-system.

The canopy opened underneath them as they lowered. They touched down and Walstib spoke again, "Shuttle bus. Hangar canopy. Close please."

They climbed down the ladder and walked back to the glass elevator as the hangar canopy closed above them. Walstib and Mae strode forward quickly being accustomed to the massive structure moving overhead. The Sci Team, however, kept looking up and felt as if they had to duck even though the hangar canopy was three stories above them.

They rode the elevator back up to the observation level.

CHAPTER 21

Back in the observation level at Walstib's lab, everyone slumped down on some very comfy overstuffed Brazilian leather sofas. They all just sat and closed their eyes. It had been a whirlwind day.

Walstib posed another question, "Let's put the question of the spiders aside for the moment. What do we make of this AUCO?"

Ellie looked thoughtful, then happy, "How about American University, in Washington, DC? I have a friend going there. What if they are doing research on bio-diversity in the rainforest?"

Walstib thought for a minute, "I know academic competition for research grants can get pretty intense but these poachers tying up Althea was over the top. I'd say we have to rule that out."

Yang said, "What if it is simply short for Auto Company? What if they are trying to meld spider webbing to tires for additional traction and durability?"

"I actually like that idea. If they aren't, we should," said Walstib.

Neil and Yang did an across the room high-five.

"What if it's just the owner's name or initials? It could be any one of thousands of names," suggested Anne.

Walstib frowned, "Very possible. If that's the case we may never find out."

"What if the meaning of the name doesn't matter? If we find out where they are located we can just go knock on their door and find out what they are doing?" said Neil hopefully. "Do you have Search-It down here? We can do a Search-It for their address."

Mae tilted her head and rolled her eyes toward her dad very, very subtly.

Neil looked at Mae, subtly pointed at Walstib, and mouthed, "He invented Search-It?"

She gave a quick proud smile and a quick nod.

Neil looked at Walstib.

Walstib smiled, "Yeah, we've got that. Let's give it a try." He turned to the screen, "Search-it. AUCO."

The soft voice on the computer screen responded instantly, "One listing." The screen showed: AUCO. 1003 Stella Road, Elektrostal, Russia.

"Describe Elektrostal, please."

"Elektrostal is a small town in Russia, east of Moscow. Formerly a military manufacturing town, many of the industrial buildings have been abandoned as the local community re-establishes itself as a farming region."

"Odd that there is only one listing," said Mae.

"Not if they're trying to be covert," said Yang.

"Why any listing? Why do they show up in Russia?" asked Ellie.

"All transactions in Russia now require a certificate of identification. After they became a democracy a few decades ago they went through what the media described as a 'Wild West' phase. They've matured as a country and aim to keep their top 'Ethics in Government' rating from the World Ethics Institute."

"Now what?" asked Neil.

"Sounds like we need to go knock on a door. Who likes caviar?" replied Walstib.

CHAPTER 22

"Do we get frequent flyer miles on the Shuttle Bus for our
trip to Moscow?" asked Anne.
"We'll use the Shuttle Bus for the last leg of the journey.
We'll use something faster to get most of the way. Who
wants to putter along at Mach 2?" responded Walstib.
The four looked at each other, then Yang said cheerfully,
"Well, not us."

Walstib turned to the screen and stated, "HyperRider.
Hangar canopy. Open, please."
They all followed Walstib to the right side of the building
and went into another glass elevator.
There they saw a much bigger hangar canopy than the
Shuttle Bus canopy. It was the same design as Walstib's
launch facility in the desert. The ground shook slightly. A
long strip of solar trees, about one hundred meters long by
thirty meters wide, quickly started tipping over and the
whole hangar canopy lowered about one meter then slid
sideways. A long metal launch ramp, angled slightly
upward at the far end, raised up.

The elevator took them down five stories. It opened and for
the first time the four friends were speechless. They stared
in amazement at the scramjet. Long and sleek, it just looked
fast, even standing still. Although the scramjet had wheels,
they were retracted in the launch position. The fuselage was
attached to the launch ramp.
"Is this a magnetic launch ramp?" asked Neil.

"Yes," said Walstib proudly, "it's much shorter and thus easier to conceal than a long conventional airstrip. I don't need prying eyes spotting it from the air. Corporate drones criss-cross this continent looking for my lab all the time."
"And cheaper, more energy efficient, and quieter than a launch catapult," added Neil.
"Exactly. All right let's climb aboard."
They climbed up the entrance ladder, which was slightly bigger than the Shuttle Bus ladder.
The inside was also slightly bigger with the same pilot and navigator seating but with twelve seats and a large walled off storage room aft. They sat down and buckled in, Walstib in the pilot seat, Mae next to him, and the four others behind them.
Walstib turned to the four Sci Team passengers and said with a smile, "You'll feel a bit more compression on take-off this time."

He looked forward and pushed two red buttons on the instrument panel at the same time. There was a slight whirring sound, a faint metallic un-coupling sound, then a subtle whooshing sound. And before they could even look out the windows, they were airborne. Walstib pushed a third red button and bam, the rockets kicked in. The feeling of being pushed back in their seats was much, much firmer than before. The g-force was about triple that of the take off of the Shuttle Bus.
"Is my belly button supposed to be touching my backbone?" asked Anne.

"That feeling should be easing up right about now as we stop accelerating and hit cruising speed," responded Mae. "You get used to it after a while."

"OK Yang, here is your next question," said Walstib.

"I'm ready," smiled Yang.

"Cruising speed is Mach 18, and the distance from the lab to Moscow is approximately 11,300 kilometers. How long…" Walstib hadn't even completed the question when Yang buzzed in.

"Bzzz…approximately 34 minutes."

"Last time you were exact. Why did you say approximately?"

"32 minutes is the time based strictly on distance divided by speed. But, I rounded up to take into account additional time for acceleration at take-off and deceleration at arrival."

"That's why he's on the Sci Team," beamed Ellie.

"Hmmm," said Walstib.

Walstib turned his seat around to face the four passengers. Anne raised her eyebrows in shock and pointed both her forefingers forward out the windscreen.

"Not to worry, Anne. We are now on auto-pilot. Secondly we have sensors, and thirdly no one else is up here over twenty kilometers high."

"So, Ellie," continued Walstib, "tell me about Sci Team."

"Let's see," Ellie started as she looked at her friends, "we met freshman year, we were in some of the same advanced classes, and realized we all loved science. We teamed up for some science competitions, started winning, and we just stayed with it."

"And won four straight National Science Quiz Bowls as I saw on your transcripts," finished Walstib.

"At one of the local competitions, some of our buddies on the football team and swim team held up signs that read 'Go Sci Team'. The name kind of stuck," added Anne.

"That was your moniker in high school. But after you graduated, you arrived at my doorstep in an airship, which has its own nomenclature. Wouldn't that make you all the Sci Crew?" posited Walstib.

"I like that," grinned Neil.

"I like that, too," said Ellie.

"Change is good," said Anne.

"Can I change my answer?" asked Yang.

"Of course. Science is a moving target. Every time you find an answer, it may not be *the answer*, but it may get you closer to *the answer*," said Walstib.

"Make that approximately 35 minutes."

"How so?"

"We are chasing a moving target. The Earth is rotating away from us as we fly toward our destination, so I added another minute."

"Exactly," smiled Walstib.

They looked out the windows for a minute soaking in the spectacular view of a beautiful world beneath them.

Walstib stood up and announced, "Time to de-plane."

"Awesome! Wingsuits at twenty klicks up!" said Yang as he jumped up.

Everyone just stared at him.

"No?" murmured Yang as he looked around.

"I think it's best not to announce our arrival. The HyperRider tends to attract attention, so, sorry, just another Shuttle Bus," said Walstib as he opened the pressurized door to the rear storage area.

They all entered the rear compartment and the pressurized door was sealed shut.

Walstib pushed a button on the side of the Shuttle Bus, the ladder came down, and they all clambered aboard.

Walstib, sitting in the Shuttle Bus pilot's seat spoke into the com system, "HyperRider. Reduce speed to Shuttle Bus release setting."

They felt the plane slowing down.

Seconds later a light on the instrument panel flashed and a com-system voice stated, "Speed setting achieved."

"Open bay doors." They could feel a motorized hum as the doors opened.

"Shuttle Bus. Lower." The hoists that were holding the Shuttle Bus lowered it down through the opening and the occupants could feel a slight buffeting.

"Shuttle Bus. Release please." As soon as they were released and in a free-fall, Walstib pushed a button on the joystick and pushed it forward. They shot forward under their own power.

The Sci Crew looked up through the glass canopy and could see the HyperRider bay doors fold up as the scramjet gained speed and disappeared into the distance.

"Where is it going?" asked Ellie.

"Back to the lab," said Mae, "it will hover-land back in its launch bay."

They could see the lights of Moscow beneath them as they descended quickly. Walstib steered toward Moscow's Domodedovo International Airport and as they got within a kilometer he veered to the private jet hangar section. He stated, "Hangar. Roof. Open." As they started to hover down they could see the roof parting in the middle and slide open.

CHAPTER 23

The Shuttle Bus hovered down into the private hangar, the
roof closed, and Mae pushed a button to lower the ladder.
Walstib grabbed a backpack, "Let's head out."
As they climbed down, Ellie asked, "What's in the
backpack?"
"Emergency stuff, just in case," responded Walstib.
Ellie thought it best not to ask a follow-up question.

As they finished climbing down the ladder, they turned and
saw an amazing four-wheel drive vehicle. As they had been
unconscious the first time they were in the Jungle Trekker
they didn't recognize the body style. The City Trekker was
all black and had the same oversized knobby tires.
"Hop in," said Walstib as he climbed in the driver's seat.
The others climbed in as well.
Walstib spoke into the com system, "Hangar. Car door.
Open, please."
The door rolled up and they exited the hangar. "Hangar.
Car door. Close."

They were on the back service road used by everyone or
every company that had a private hangar. It was well
maintained and well lit.

What the Sci Crew, Walstib, and Mae didn't notice was
that they were being watched. Two figures were in a
medium size black car, up on the small hill that overlooked
the private hangar section. The figures in the car were using
binoculars to observe the comings and goings.

"Once they exit the airport road, follow them," said the occupant sitting in the passenger seat.

The second occupant, the driver, watched as Walstib's car left the service road, passed through the gate, and entered the main road, the M7, heading east.

"Stay close," said the passenger.

They followed for several kilometers.

Mae was watching the map screen, which obviously had some upgrades.

"Dad, we're being followed."

"I'll speed up a little."

The other car kept up.

"Perhaps it's just a coincidence, but let's find out," suggested Walstib. "There's a light up ahead, press the red button on the lower left of the screen."

"That's new," said Mae.

The traffic light up ahead turned red.

"Mostly I prefer using the new green button," smiled Walstib.

The passenger noticed the light had turned red.

"Ah, good, a red light. Pull up on their left."

Both cars came to a stop at the light. Walstib rolled his window down as did Anne who was sitting behind him.

The window on the passenger side of the tailing car rolled down.

The passenger held a big camera and put on a big smile, "I apologize, I don't recognize you."

"We're just visiting," said Walstib in a flat tone.

More smiling, "Good, good, we're delighted you're here. But who are you?"

"We're just tourists."

By now all four in the back were craning to see out.

"You're not in the movies?"

"No."

"You're not on TV?"

"No."

Now the passenger was getting slightly agitated, "You've got to be somebody. You've got a private hanger, a private car…and," he pointed to the four in the back seat, "and you've got an entourage for goodness sake."

"Sorry."

He lowered his camera, "I'm on deadline to get pictures of celebrities. I stake out the airport all night, and all I get is a nobody." His window rolled up.

Walstib looked at Mae, and laughingly said, "Time to push the green button."

She pushed it and the light turned green.

The paparazzi's car pulled a U-turn and sped back to the airport.

Walstib, Mae, and the Sci Crew continued heading east on the M7.

CHAPTER 24

They continued along the M7.

Yang asked, "What if that guy had taken a picture? You said you like to keep a low profile."

"The car emits a minimal electromagnetic shield that cancels all audio and video surveillance," responded Walstib.

"Radar, too?" asked Neil.

"Radar, too."

"Now we know what to make Neil for his birthday present," winked Anne.

Everyone in the back settled into their seats, happy to relax and close their eyes, even if only for a short while.

They had driven another ten minutes when Mae saw something up ahead.

"Dad, look to the right," said Mae quietly.

Walstib slowed down slightly as they passed a side road, an ordinary, simple, dirt road. Except one thing wasn't so ordinary, a large truck with the letters AUCO on the side was waiting to turn onto the M7.

"We have to let them pass us, but I can't just pull over, it will look too suspicious," said Walstib.

Mae looked around, "There's a diner up on the left."

They pulled into the parking lot and came to a stop parallel to the road.

"Tracking screen please," said Walstib to the com-system.

The navigation screen instantly turned into a night vision video screen.

"Laser. Ready. Tracker. Ready."

The stopping, or lack of motion, woke up everyone in the back. A short ride it had been.

"What's going on?" asked Neil, sleepily.

Mae turned and smiled at everyone in the back.

"I've added a few options of my own design," said Walstib. They're selling pretty well in the law enforcement market." A small slot on the hood of the City Trekker slid open and two tubes, the size of straws, hinged up and locked in place. The AUCO truck sped by.

"Laser. Lock. Tracker. Launch," commanded Walstib.

The imperceptible black laser locked onto the passing truck and the tracker launched with a barely visible wisp of vapor from a compressed air canister.

"Laser. Conceal. Tracker. Conceal."

The two tubes hinged back under the hood.

"We saw an AUCO truck and we're tracking it," said Mae.

"Wouldn't they feel something hit the truck?" asked Neil.

"The tracking device is imbedded in a sticky aerogel. It's too light to feel even if it hit a human. And once the road dust covers it, they won't see it either," responded Walstib.

"Should we go back to see where the truck came from?" asked Anne.

"Yes," said Walstib, and after a slight pause, "however, there may be other trucks coming. Let's not get into a confrontation just yet. We can follow the tracking device later on the GPS."

Yang pointed to the diner, "Maybe we could grab a bite to eat in there, sit by the window, and watch to see if any more trucks come by."

Everyone nodded in agreement. Walstib pulled the City Trekker up to the front of the diner and they all piled out.

The sign above the door read 'Good Chow'. Walstib said, "That's either very good or very bad."

Once seated in a window booth, they all stared out the window.

The server came over to describe the specials. Half the time the six were listening and half the time they kept looking out the window.

"I've never been to Russia before," said Ellie.

"Me neither," said Anne.

The other two shook their heads.

"What would you recommend?" asked Walstib, despite clearly having been to Russia multiple times.

"How about a cup of borshch for everyone, several plates of pirozhkis, and several plates of blinis with caviar?"

"Splendid," smiled Walstib.

The server went back to order the food and the six went back to looking out the window.

No one spoke.

After a few minutes, the server brought out the food, which looked delicious.

"I hope you like the food, my husband is the cook. He was formerly on Iron Chef St. Petersburg," she said proudly.

"Why are you staring out the window? We have no view, it's just a road, not a golden road, just a road."

"We are being stalked by the paparazzi. They think we're on TV," gushed Mae.

"Well, you're a good looking family," said the server.

"Especially you," as she pinched Walstib's cheek.

"I heard that," said the husband from the kitchen.

"But you need to add a little weight." She turned to look at the entire table, "You all need to add a little weight. Eat up, eat up!"

They all looked at her and smiled.

As she turned to walk away, Ellie, who was sitting closest to the window, looked back out the window, and abruptly tapped the table and blurted a very muted, "Look, look, look."

They all turned to watch as ten more large AUCO trucks lumbered by.

Walstib said, "So they sent a lookout truck first, then the main convoy. There should be a follow-up truck coming behind them. Let's keep an eye out."

The food was as delicious as it looked and they ate quickly and silently except for appreciative nods and smiles. As they were finishing, the server came over to re-fill their water glasses.

Walstib engaged her with a smile, "As tourists, we have seen a lot of the big cities, but sometimes we like to travel off the beaten path. We noticed a dirt road back there" and he pointed in the direction where they had just passed, "does it lead anywhere?"

"Nothing. Just an old abandoned nuclear plant."

"Thank you," said Walstib as he put his fingerprint on the billing tablet.

They all thanked her and left the diner. They saw one last AUCO truck speed by as they got in the City Trekker. "Time for a tour," said Walstib.

CHAPTER 25

They headed back west on the M7 for a kilometer or so until they spotted the dirt road. There was no sign, had they not seen the AUCO truck before, there was nothing there that would indicate there was anything off the main road. They turned left and slowly made their way down the straight flat road, perhaps well maintained some years earlier. They got to the end and there were tall, chain-link security fences, but, much to their surprise, the gates were wide open.

Walstib spoke to the com system, "Map close. Geiger counter on."

The GPS map blinked off and the screen showed the graph of a Geiger counter.

They all leaned forward and looked at the Geiger counter screen: nothing.

Walstib turned off the headlights, there was enough moonlight to see. They drove forward slowly through the open gates and came to a Gothic architecture inspired stone guard house. The drop down security arm was in the down position. Walstib stopped the Trekker, and they all got out. Walstib grabbed his backpack. As they walked past the arm, they came to what would have been the front of the nuclear plant, a massive structure of concrete and steel. But instead, nothing. Walstib pulled a flashlight out of his backpack and shined the light straight out. Nothing except hectares of dirt.

They continued to walk forward slowly when very bright lights snapped on and a metallic, bullhorn voice barked "Halt."

Walstib and the others were blinded and stopped abruptly.

"Who's there?" continued the bullhorn voice.

"Just tourists," offered Walstib.

Silence.

Yang spoke up, "A rock group really. We're scouting out locations for a video."

The bullhorn continued, "What's the name of your group?"

"Sci Crew."

"Never heard of you."

"We're new, we're an independent band," continued Yang.

"I've heard of every new independent rock group. How do I know you're really in the music scene?"

"Quiz us," boasted Yang

"What do you think of Long Gray Line?"

"They're cool. But they're not new, they've been around for years," answered Neil.

"What do you think of Max Q?"

"We love them, although a bit cosmic," answered Anne.

"What about Beast Barracks?"

"Good, they make you think, but a bit abrasive," added Ellie.

Silence.

"You sound legit," said a slightly softer bullhorn.

The lights snapped off and they could then, once their eyes readjusted to the dark, see by the moonlight that the light had come from a row of high beam spotlights on top of a large construction truck. Out of the truck jumped down a short, slender man, who looked to be in his eighties.

Despite the darkness you could still tell he had intelligent, twinkling eyes.

"Dr. Fissile?" asked Walstib.

"Why yes," replied Fissile, rather surprised. He squinted, put on his glasses, stared, then smiled. "Wally?"

"Of course old friend."

"I haven't seen you since Davos. When did you grow a beard?"

"A few years ago."

"It looks good. When did you become an independent rock group manager?"

"About two minutes ago. But," looking at Mae and the Sci Crew, "it sounds like fun."

"So what are you really doing here?"

"We're trying to figure out what AUCO is up to. We saw them torching parts of the rain forest in order to poach spiders. And we got a lead that they are operating in Russia."

"Maybe it's a different company," suggested Dr. Fissile.

"The trucks coming out of here had the same logo as the trucks in Brazil."

"Still, hard to think they're the same company. They're the biggest recycling company in Russia. Ever since we switched our grid to all renewables, thanks to you," Fissile said with a smile and a nod, "AUCO has been dismantling and recycling all the old nuclear plants."

"Are you working for them?"

"No, no. I'm still paid by the plant. Since I designed the plant, I was asked to oversee the demolition and certify that it's completely shut down."

"It looks way past shut down, it looks gone. We didn't detect any radiation at all coming in."

"It's completely gone. That was the last convoy out."

Neil made a slight cough, "What was in the last convoy?"

"The last of the nuclear material."

"Why did they ship it at night?" Neil continued.

"They told me they were asked to take the nuclear material out at night to keep those along the exit route from getting worried."

"Where are they taking it?"

"One of the central long-term storage facilities. Don't know specifically. They had to remove it from here since we had no storage capabilities. They've done a good job of scrubbing the place, as you noted, no nuclear signature. I think the new owner is going to build condos here. That's why they left the guard gate, a little historic flair for the new community."

Walstib put his hand on Neil's shoulder, a gentle signal to bring this line of questioning to an end.

"What are you going to do next?" Walstib asked.

"Nothing. As you know, after *The Incident*, all nuclear weapons and nuclear power plants were outlawed internationally and we have been diverting all the nuclear material to ultra secure storage facilities. I was interested in transferring the material into long-range space exploration vehicles, but budget cuts wiped out that program. So, to answer your question, I may, at age 88 be forced to retire."

"You've earned a long and happy retirement. It was good to see you again. We're going to push on and see what we can find out about AUCO."

"Good seeing you too. Here, take this." He handed Walstib a small device. "This will read the signature from my nuclear material. It's much more fine-tuned than any generic Geiger counter. I won't be needing it anymore. I hope my material is going where it's supposed to go. Farewell old friend."

They shook hands warmly.

Fissile climbed back into his truck. Walstib, Mae, and the Sci Crew turned to walk back to their Trekker.

All of a sudden, the lights snapped back on and the bullhorn barked, "Hey Sci Crew…"

Walstib and Mae turned around. The Sci Crew froze.

The bullhorn continued, "If you ever cut a few songs, let me know."

CHAPTER 26

They left the old plant entrance road, turned right, and again headed east on M7. As they passed the diner, Mae readjusted the screen to show the GPS map.

From the back, Ellie asked, "How did you meet Dr. Fissile?"

"We first met at an energy conference in Geneva a little over twenty-five years ago. The last time was in Davos. Brilliant man. We stayed in touch for years, but shifting my lab to Brazil took a lot of time and I fell out of touch with many friends." Walstib looked at Mae, "I need to reconnect with some old friends, maybe throw a party or something."

Mae smiled and said softly, "Good idea."

After a few minutes of silence, Anne asked, "How does Dr. Fissile know so much about rock music?"

Walstib laughed, "One. Does it look as if there is anything else to do out here? And, two. What other kind of music is worth listening to?"

Ellie smiled and said, "Good point."

Mae turned to face the others in the back of the Trekker, "Are you really in a rock group?"

"No," said Yang sheepishly.

"Yang, don't you play drums?" asked Ellie.

"I took lessons for a few years."

"I didn't know that," said Neil. "Ellie, do you play anything?"

"A little piano," responded Ellie.

"You mean a little piano like the tiny ones the clowns play in the circus?" laughed Anne as she tried to give Ellie a playful poke.

"Hey," said Ellie as she contorted away, "what do you play?"

"A little guitar."

"You mean a ukulele?" shot back Ellie while trying to poke back at Anne.

As they continued poking at each other and laughing, Neil turned to the two in the back and gestured to calm down. The two looked directly at him and Anne said, "Well, what do *you* play?"

"I practiced playing a regular, normal, standard size guitar for several years." Trying to divert attention from himself, Neil turned to the front and quickly added, "What about you Mae?"

"I used to sing in the chorus in school before we moved to the new lab."

"Sounds like we have a group," said Walstib. "Remember, as manager, I get ten percent."

They laughed.

"You know," continued Walstib, "many parents sign their kids up for music lessons hoping it will help in math."

"Is it true? Does that really work?" asked Yang.

"Well obviously," said Walstib with a knowing grin.

"Hold on," said Mae as she looked at the GPS map, "we're getting close."

CHAPTER 27

They passed a small road sign stating, "Welcome to Elektrostal". Mostly what they saw was farmland.

Mae was studiously watching the GPS. "Slow down a little…the AUCO address is up ahead. Take the next right," whispered Mae. "OK, now go about half a kilometer."

Everyone in the back leaned forward.

They had entered a sprawling warehouse district. Everything looked new and clean, but there were no people, trucks, cars, or streetlights. None of the buildings had lights on, except several massive buildings toward the end of the street, which were partially lit.

Mae was looking at the numbers on the first buildings. "The big buildings down there are the AUCO buildings," whispered Mae.

Walstib brought the Trekker to a slow crawl several blocks short of the AUCO buildings, then pulled into a side street and stopped.

Walstib looked at Mae, "Can you please check on the tracking device on the back of the AUCO truck?"

Mae pushed a few buttons, the tracking signal came up on the GPS screen.

"The tracking device signal is coming from the AUCO warehouse."

Walstib grabbed his backpack, "Let's take a very careful walk to the plant."

They all got out, closed the doors quietly, and started walking down the alleyway very cautiously. As they got closer to the facility they could hear the sounds of heavy trucks, metal gates clanging, and men shouting. As they reached the end of the alleyway they stopped.

Walstib peaked around the corner of the building very briefly. He then reached into his backpack and pulled out a small set of binoculars.

"There's a row of trucks. It's a little darker here than back at the old nuclear plant and it's hard to make out much detail. These night vision binoculars should help."

Before he could turn back to look, Neil put his hand on the binoculars and said, "I've got this."

Slightly surprised, Walstib said, "OK."

Neil took the binos and lay belly down on the street. He inched his way forward till he just barely could see around the corner. He held up the binos and surveyed the exterior of the plant and the trucks. The others looked at each other in approval.

Neil backed up, stood up, and handed the binos back to Walstib. "Thought we'd be less obvious from that position."

"Good idea. What did you see?"

"A barbed wire perimeter fence around the facility. A long procession of old military type trucks with canvas covers going into the facility one at a time. All the trucks had AUCO printed on the side. And several uniformed security guards at the gate."

"We need a closer look," said Walstib, as he reached into his backpack and pulled out a small plastic box. He opened the box, which was generously padded inside, and gently picked up a tiny FlyCam as well as the screen and joystick controller. He pushed the button on the FlyCam and released it upward. He maneuvered the joystick and sent the Fly up and over the warehouse building.

Everyone craned to see the screen as the Fly sent back ultra clear visuals.

Walstib deftly moved the stick forward slightly, "I'll make a quick flyover…no pun intended."

They all saw the fencing, the guards, and what must have been over a hundred trucks lined up.

Anne asked eagerly, "Can we see what's in the trucks?"

"Hopefully, if one has a loose flap."

Walstib circled the Fly back for a slower flyby. The Fly hovered over one truck, then the next.

Ellie pointed, "There's an opening. There on the back of truck number four from the rear."

Walstib lowered the Fly and guided it slowly into the truck. On the screen they saw several large plastic drums.

"Looks like lettering on the side of the drums," said Ellie, whose eyes were fixed on the screen.

"Good catch," said Yang, "it's really dark in there."

The Fly moved closer to the drums. Into view came the words, stenciled in block letters: SPIDER WEBBING.

"Well now we know this is the same company that was in Brazil," said Yang.

"We have to be very cautious with these people," said Walstib, in a rather fatherly tone.

"I hope they didn't take enough spiders to fill all these trucks," said Mae.

Anne nodded to Mae, "Can you check some other trucks?"

"Let's see," said Walstib slowly as he eased the Fly out of the truck.

The fly moved up the line of trucks slowly, pausing momentarily at the back flap of each truck. Another opening. In the Fly went.

"Steel drums," said Ellie. "Oh no," she gasped under breath.

They all could see this sign, in yellow, the international symbol for nuclear material.

"This looks all wrong," said Walstib, sounding slightly annoyed. "Why would they have the nuclear material here? This is a warehouse district near a small town, nowhere near a long-term storage facility."

"Dr. Fissile is going to be pissed," whispered Anne.

"Keep checking other trucks," exhorted Neil. "Please," he quickly added.

"This is a pretty weird combo as it is. What else could there be?" said Mae.

The fatherly tone again, "Agreed, but just the same, let's check some more. Best to know all the facts."

The Fly moved on. Passing another truck and another and another. Finally an opening, and in it went.

"OK," said Mae, "it just got weirder."

On the screen they could see a section of a rocket from the space program.

CHAPTER 28

Walstib looked at Mae and the Sci Crew, "If this is for a government contract to launch spider webbing into space to catch space debris, this is being a little too secretive. What could they be doing?"
Blank stares.
Walstib muttered to himself, "What time is it in Hawaii?" as he pulled out his com-phone. "Contact Dr. Chondrule, please."

The observatory tour guide, pleasant looking in a lab coat, with a strong voice, was giving the usual morning tour. "This way please. Gather 'round. Good morning. The Keck Observatory is the largest optical telescope observatory in the world. The observatory is headed by the preeminent astrophysicist Dr. Chondrule, who has spotted more new comets and asteroids than any other stargazer. Now, if you'll follow me, over here on my left...."

Upstairs, away from the tour group, was Dr. Chondrule's office, cluttered with numerous awards, plaques, and mementoes. His favorite, hanging on the wall behind him, was an antique original movie poster of ET signed by Steven Spielberg. Dr. Chondrule was sitting on a stool, staring into the eyepiece of a very, very large telescope. Dr. Chondrule hears the com system ring, looks up at the com screen, and sees the word 'Wally' scroll across.
"Accept call." Walstib's face shows up on the screen.
"Hello Wally, good to hear from you,"
Chondrule said excitedly.

"Hello, Dr. Chondrule. What's new?"

"Nothing, everything in our universe is 13 billion years old."

"That's my favorite joke of yours."

"That's my only joke. What's up?"

"We have a potential problem on our hands and we need your help. Specifically, what in space could have extraordinarily high value? And, something so far away it would take nuclear rockets to reach."

Dr. Chondrule took a few steps over to his computer, sat down, and typed into the computer.

"Let me check here. Ah, yes. Looking under the category 'composition' there was a sighting that was listed in 1994 that is almost all gold."

Walstib puts his hand over the phone and whispers to the others, "AUCO stands for gold."

Everyone else grimaces, knowing they should have realized that Au is the symbol for gold on the periodic table of the elements. The capital u threw them off.

"How can you be sure of the asteroid's content?" asked Walstib.

"It's not an asteroid, surprisingly, it's a comet, which as you know is mostly covered with ice. There are a variety of telescopes to determine the composition, including gamma ray, infrared, microwave, optical, radio, ultraviolet, and x-ray. Each one provides a different picture of the object. Separately you might miss something. Used together they're quite accurate."

"Why didn't this make the news?"

"It didn't receive much attention for several reasons. One, it was very far away. And secondly, it was logged-in at the

International Astronomical Union at the same time as the sighting of Comet Shoemaker-Levy which got all the attention because it had that spectacular collision with Jupiter. For a short time, it didn't even have a name, we just called it 'the other one'. And thirdly, its composition is not that unusual."

"Gold isn't unusual?"

"Everything in the Universe, the planets, comets, asteroids, etc., all originated from the same common elements. It's not unusual for asteroids or comets to have other elements besides rock as part of their make-up....nickel and sulfur for example. Many asteroids contain iron. In fact, the early Native Americans used iron from fallen meteorites to make tools."

"How could there be a comet that size with gold as the predominant element?"

"In our Galaxy, there are millions of planets many times the size of our planet, Jupiter and Saturn in our own solar system for instance. Imagine a planet hundreds of times bigger than the Earth breaking up because it was hit by another planet. The Earth's gold can be mere nuggets or veins maybe an inch thick. But a gigantic planet, if it broke up, could let loose gold veins or nuggets tens of meters thick. Metallic asteroids are rare but not uncommon."

"How large is this one?"

Dr. Chondrule looked again in the computer, "Let's check the listing. Oh, it is a medium size. Approximately five kilometers in diameter, but the gold core is about fifty meters in diameter."

"How much would that weigh? Just the gold?"

"There's probably millions of tonnes of ice surrounding the gold core." Typing into the computer as he spoke, "Let's say a core of fifty meters in diameter. Input four thirds Pi r cubed, the volume of a sphere…times the density of gold, which is 19 grams per cubic centimeter. And…" Chondrule hit one final key on the keyboard, "900,000 tonnes of gold!"

"And what is today's price of gold?"

"Wally what's this all about? Aren't you in your office?"

"I am definitely not in my office. That's all I can say right now. I'll buy you a new telescope if that will help."

"You don't need to do that." Chondrule typed again into his computer. "Ah, 500 WUs per gram."

"So how much is this comet worth?"

"Let's see….the weight of the comet," more typing into the computer, "times price of gold is…"

"450 trillion WUs," whispered Yang.

"Good gracious……450 trillion WUs," said Chondrule.

"Wow. So even if someone spent billions of WUs retrieving the comet, they would still make a huge profit."

"Better than the profit on my savings account at the bank. But what do you mean by retrieving it?"

"What if someone wanted to catch this comet, bring it to earth, and mine it for the gold?"

"That may make perfect financial sense for some businessperson. However, there are many reasons why this would be a disaster for the rest of us. If he or she wants to park the comet in orbit in order to mine it, it might be close enough to change the climate and ruin all the crops for decades. Or it could disrupt the tides and wipe out all the

coastal cities. Or, if they can't keep it in orbit and the comet is caught by Earth's gravity and pulled……."
As Chondrule paused, Walstib added, "This comet is about the same size of the one that killed off the dinosaurs. It could destroy everything on the planet."
Chondrule continued, "Wally, you can't let this happen."
Walstib, not quite sure how to be reassuring, could just muster, "Thanks for the info, gotta sign off, will check in later," and hung up.
Walstib looked at the others who looked very nervous.
Anne grimaced, "We can't let this happen."
"We won't," said Walstib.

CHAPTER 29

Walstib looked earnestly at Mae and the Sci Crew, "I'm not just saying that, I think we can stop them."

They all looked slightly relieved.

"OK, so what we have here is Dr. Fissile's nuclear material, rocket parts, and spider webbing. What do we know about spider webbing?"

Neil, Anne, and Yang all looked at Ellie.

Ellie looked at the others, then at Walstib with an inquisitive look.

Walstib looked directly at Ellie, "I know a lot about a lot, but I don't know everything."

Ellie looked a little unsure but started, "All right. I'll give the short version. Spider silk in general is the most amazing fiber on the planet. It's several times stronger than steel, several times more flexible than nylon or Kevlar, and it's waterproof. Some small spiders can shoot out silk at a meter per second for eight hours at a time. And the particular spiders that the AU Company were collecting are the largest in Brazil, and the largest by weight, on Earth. They may be trying to build the world's largest spider web to catch that asteroid."

"Will spider webbing withstand the cold of space?"

"I've never seen any research articles on that issue." Ellie thought that if she had said that sentence in school she might have been laughed at, however, she felt almost like a colleague saying that to Walstib.

Neil looked at Ellie to make sure she had finished, then commented, "Speaking of research makes me think of research funding. Whoever these folks are, this project has got to be costing them a lot of money."

"Good point," said Walstib. He opened his com-phone again, "Contact Russian President Tereshkova."

Everyone looked a bit surprised.

An official sounding assistant answered, "President Tereshkova's private line."

"Dr. Walstib calling, President Tereshkova please."

"She's asleep, Sir."

"I think she'll want to take this call."

"Sir, I shouldn't say this, but, it's very late and she's just fallen asleep. It's not life or death is it?"

The others had been listening in and were emphatically nodding their heads.

"It is," said Walstib somberly.

"Just a moment."

After a long thirty seconds, President Tereshkova answered, "Wally! What's up, besides me?"

"Sorry to wake you. Actually I thought you'd still be up partying."

"Not to worry. I was out late last night, that's why I had to turn in at two tonight. What can I do for you?"

We may have uncovered a slight problem in your backyard. I am hoping that you can do a financial and background check on a company operating in Russia under the name AUCO or AU Company."

"Au as in gold?"

Everyone rolled their eyes or shook their head sheepishly.

"Exactly," said Walstib trying not to sound chagrined.

"Anything I should know about this?"

"We think the owner of this company might be jeopardizing the planet merely for financial gain."

"What's wrong with these people? When is enough, enough?"

"I know. Things are out of hand. But, we're on this."

"All right, I'll get my people on this too, right now."

"Thank you. Just please keep the inquiries as low profile as possible," said Walstib. They both hung up. "That may take a while. These guys don't look as if they're listed with the Better Business Bureau."

"I was thinking that they might just be building a prototype," suggested Mae, "but this seems too big to be just a research project."

"We can't let them do this," Anne repeated in a determined voice.

"Agreed," said Walstib. "We'd better go inside and have a look around. We need a way to get past the guards."

"Maybe we could wait till all the trucks are inside and the guards might go in with them," suggested Ellie.

"By then it might be light outside and they'd see us," cautioned Yang. He peeked around the corner of the building. "The guards don't seem to be inspecting the trucks too closely as they go through the gates. I guess they figure 'Who would be out here?' Maybe we should try to sneak through in one of the trucks."

"I'll send the Fly around back and see if there is a back door," said Walstib in a tone that suggested a measured approach might be more appropriate.

"I'm sure there's a back door," said Anne flatly. "Do we have a key?"

"Well, no," said Walstib equally flatly.

"Well, let's get truckin'," said Anne in a newly spirited tone. She peeked around the corner, saw no guards, sprinted to the back of the last truck, unlatched the back flap, and dove into the truck.

Horrified, Walstib looked around the corner, then back at the others, "She's really fast. Impetuous, but fast."

Neil looked at Walstib, "I guess we're going in?"

Walstib looked at Neil, "I guess we are." He looked around the corner to make sure the coast was clear, ready to signal the next person to make the dash to the truck. Instead, what he saw were two burly guards who had walked to the end of the line of trucks.

CHAPTER 30

Charlie Leake sat in a big chair behind a big desk in his make-shift office on the third and top floor of the warehouse in Russia. He had just flown in from New York and was anxious to move his new project forward.

The Warehouse Facilities Manager, a burly man who looked like a former security guard, knocked on the door, "Mr. Charlie? It's Frank Tower."

"Come in."

The door opened and Frank strode purposefully over to Charlie Leake's desk.

"The last of the trucks have arrived."

"Good. Thank you for handling this phase so promptly. I will be turning over all the material to the technicians for the next phase, but I want you to stay around and help."

"Thank you, but why do you need me for the next phase?"

"I want to speed things up and I'll need you to assist with organizing double shifts."

"Double shifts? Won't that exhaust the technicians?"

"Do I look like I care?"

"I'm happy to be of assistance. But why the rush?"

"Competition. I need to stay ahead of the competition."

"Nobody knows about your project."

"There's always competition."

"Don't worry Boss. Nobody knows anything."

CHAPTER 31

In a small non-descript government office in the center of
Moscow, a small non-descript government worker, with the
illustrious title of 'Minister of Corporate Financial
Research', made a phone call. His twentieth call that night.
A tall, sharp looking manager was walking down a long
row of steel drums marked with the nuclear symbol. He had
a hand-held e-check pad and was marking off each drum on
the check-list. The main com-system rang and rolled over
to his com-phone.

"Storage Facility Seven, Night Manager speaking."

"This is Minister Esau."

"Good evening, Minister."

"Have all the drums been delivered to your facility?"

"All were accounted for when they were delivered. I am
almost done with a duplicate check now that they are inside
the facility."

"Do you detect any radiation?"

The Night Manager pulled out his portable Geiger-counter.

"No, Sir."

"Isn't that unusual?"

"Not with the new drums."

"Pop one of the tops."

"Sir?"

"Pop one of the tops."

The Night Manager punched in a code on one of the drums
and the automated hinge on the lid hissed open. He looked
inside.

"It's empty, Sir."

"Not to worry. I think the mix-up is on our end. Don't say a word to anyone. I'll take care of this."

The Minister hung up.

The Minister made another call.

"Yes?" a deep voice answered.

"Hello, General, this is …"

"No names over the phone, I recognize your voice," said the General.

"You said to call if anything came up that sounded interesting."

"Yes, I remember."

"I was asked to do some financial research on a company here in Russia." A pause. "You also said you'd pay me three percent of any deal that I help you with."

"Yes, I remember that also."

"OK, sorry, just wanted to make sure."

"Go on," said the General in a low voice.

"A certain local company has been spending billions of WUs, which by itself doesn't raise any red flags. They also have the contract to secure the nuclear material from the old nuclear power plants, which by itself doesn't raise any red flags. They have collected all the material, which by itself doesn't raise any red flags. However, the material hasn't arrived at any of our certified storage facilities. If this is some sort of rogue extremist group, you'll have to take them out. My hope is that this is merely a sloppy business venture that is not completing their contract, in which case I thought you might be able to extract some sort of hefty fine."

"I like your idea."

"I have an address."
"E-mail it to me and I'll round up some colleagues and some *persuasive* equipment to assist in extracting the fine."

CHAPTER 32

Walstib looked back at Neil, "I guess we're not going in. Two guards just showed up."

The two guards stopped at the last truck, the older guard said to the younger guard, "See? Nothing. This is your first assignment and you're just eager to see something. You want to be the hero and move up the ladder and take my job. Not gonna happen. Now get back to the gate and stop causing a fuss."

Neil took a peek, "They're leaving. I can't leave Anne by herself."

Walstib reached into his backpack and pulled out two tubes, giving them to Neil. "Once you're in the truck spray this one on both of you. And this one is for emergencies." He looked around the corner, the street was again empty of guards. He looked at Neil, "Go."

Neil sprinted to the truck and dove in.

Anne gave Neil a big grin and asked, "Are the others coming too?"

"I think so," smiled Neil.

Just then, the truck lurched forward. The line of trucks moved forward about one hundred meters as the first few trucks had passed inspection and crossed through the gate. "I don't think so," grimaced Neil.

Upon hearing the trucks moving, Mae looked around the corner, "We may have missed our chance."

Walstib was still holding the Fly controller. He pushed the 'On' button again. He spoke to the few remaining members of his team, "The Fly lands and goes into sleep mode to conserve energy if it isn't getting a command signal. Let's see if there's a back entrance."

CHAPTER 33

Inside the truck, Anne and Neil nestled behind big steel
drums marked with the nuclear symbol.

"What now?" asked Anne.

"Wally said to spray this on once we got in the truck." He
pulled out the tube which upon closer inspection looked
like a small aerosol canister.

Anne looked perplexed, "Is this perfume? Is he giving us a
hint?" She smelled under her arms.

"You smell fine."

"Maybe it is perfume and he wants me to use my feminine
wiles on the guards inside."

"No, he said for us both to spray this on."

"Both? I hate to break this to you, but you ain't got no
feminine wiles." She poked him.

"Glad to hear that. All right, come on, let me spray you."

Anne frowned, "What's it going to do?"

"I don't know, but with 1,802 patents I suppose he knows
what he's doing."

"On the other hand, we're sitting next to drums of nuclear
material in the middle of Russia."

Neil nodded and pursed his lips, "I know. But I trust him."
The truck lurched forward again.

"I trust you." Anne leaned over and kissed Neil. "Spray
me."

Neil blushed and was about to say something, but Anne
shook her head and gestured for him to hurry up. Neil
pointed the canister at Anne and pushed down the button. A
red beam of light flashed on Anne followed by a puff of
fine mist. The light beam stopped after the puff of mist

came out. Neil stopped pointing the can and held it by his side. Nothing happened.

"That's it?" asked Anne.

Before Neil could respond, the mist moved forward, flowing to where the red beam had landed on Anne. Once it had touched her, it quickly enveloped her. Anne was completely invisible.

"Yeah, that's it," grinned Neil. "I can't see you at all."

"Wow," Anne held out her arm, covered in mist, "I can't see my arm, but I can see you. *Come on down to your local Smart Mart Tech Shop and get a can of Inviso-Mist*," Anne mimicked the ad for the national chain of high tech stores. The truck stopped.

"Quick, spray me," whispered Neil.

CHAPTER 34

At the gate, the truck slowed down then stopped. The first guard looked under the truck with a mirror, "No problem," and waved to the gate guard. The second guard opened the rear flap, looked at the steel drums and then directly at Anne and Neil. He closed the flap, shouted, "All clear," and waved to the gate guard. The gate guards opened the gate, the truck passed through the gate and then through open industrial-size doors under a sign marked "Delivery."

Once inside the facility, the truck slowed and Anne and Neil jumped off the truck. Obviously not yet used to being invisible, they hide behind a huge stack of plastic drums marked "Spider Webbing." The truck came to a stop and workers from the facility began unloading.

Neil looked at Anne, or where he knew she was crouching, "I think we should think of this as we would for any scientific endeavor, the first step being data collection."
Anne nodded, not thinking that Neil couldn't see her, "Let's find a good place for observation"
Neil stood up slowly, still getting used to being invisible, "This building is huge inside. All the floor space is blocked off into separate areas, but up there is a cat walk that goes the length of the building."
"Up where?"
"Don't you see where I'm pointing?"
"Neil, no. You're invisible."

"This may take some getting used to. Go ahead and stand up and look to your right. There is a set of metal stairs that leads to a cat walk."

Anne stood up, still cautiously, and looked to the right, "Let's go up there and have a look."

They walked carefully around the drums and past the trucks to the stairwell. They climbed slowly so as not to make any clanking sounds on the metal steps. Once they reached the top of the stairs they stopped and could see the entire Delivery area filled with a long line of trucks in the process of unloading.

"Let's see where this takes us," said Anne in a whisper. They walked slowly forward, almost tip-toeing. In the next area they could see uniformed workers carefully inserting nuclear rods into rocket engines, under a large banner that read 'Engine Assembly'.

"They're adding nuclear fuel rods into the rocket engines. The tolerances look fairly loose," whispered Neil.

"Maybe the configuration only has to last a short while. Maybe it's not being built for multiple launches."

"Still, it looks pretty unstable. I would hope that it would survive one launch. I wonder if this is how Dr. Fissile would have designed it?"

"Send him a picture," suggested Anne.

"Great idea," Neil took out his com-phone and took a picture. Typed in Dr. Fissile's name with the message: 'tolerances look loose...what do u think?' He hit send.

"Let's keep looking," said Anne.

They continued to tip-toe along the open corridor until they stood over another area with a large banner that read 'Web Assembly'. They looked over the railing and saw more uniformed workers un-coiling spider webbing from the plastic drums into a spooling mechanism.

"They must have kilometers of spider silk," said Neil.

"I wonder how many spiders survived the process," scoffed Anne.

They continued along.

In the next area, under a large banner that read 'Rocket Assembly', they saw uniformed workers inserting the nuclear rocket engines and web spooling mechanisms into the rockets.

"These rockets look like they are almost ready," said Anne.

"Hold on," Neil could feel a slight vibration on his com-phone. He opened it and gave a muffled laugh.

"What?"

"It's from Fissile. He says the engines won't survive one launch, but that 'Loose Tolerances' would make a good name for a rock group."

Anne snickered.

CHAPTER 35

"It's been several minutes and we haven't heard from them," said Ellie, sounding slightly worried.

"You guys seem pretty resourceful," responded Walstib, trying to sound upbeat. "There, the Fly is almost around the far corner of the building…let's see if there is a door along the back wall.

"Back up," blurted Yang. He pointed at the screen.

Walstib maneuvered the Fly backward.

"See, there, the faint outline of a door."

There was no door trim, no overhang, no light.

"Obviously they don't want anyone to think there's a door there. But they tried to save money by not putting a fence all around the perimeter, just around the front where it's obvious there's a door.…Let's hover down a bit…OK, there's a lock…good, it's a key lock."

"It's good it's a key lock? We don't have a key," sulked Ellie.

"Not to worry. Let's go around back," said Walstib.

He put the screen back in his backpack, hoisted it over his shoulder, looked at Mae, Yang, and Ellie, "Let's move out."

After a quick peek around the corner to make sure there were no more guards, they left their hiding spot, and half crouching, walked quickly across the street. Once they were hidden by the side wall of the AU facility, they stood up as they continued to walk.

"Dad," whispered Mae.

"Yes?" responded Walstib.

"You did it again."

"What?"

"Let's move out. Really?"

"Oh, sorry."

Ellie looked at Mae with an inquisitive look.

"He loves to watch old military movies, and sometimes he slips in a little of the jargon."

"Those guys were extraordinarily brave," protested Walstib.

"But your favorite is 'Francis Goes to'…"

Walstib held up a hand, cutting her off, as they reached the end of that side of the building. They stopped and Walstib peeked around the corner. No guards.

Walstib looked at Mae, "How's this? 'Gosh, I don't see any guards, let's go.' "

"Better," grinned Mae.

They moved around the corner and walked quickly.

Walstib motioned for Yang to go first, "You have better eyes. Look for that door."

Yang slowed down a bit and looked carefully for the barely visible door outline. He saw it and moved his hand up to let the others know to stop.

Walstib pulled off his backpack and pulled out the control screen. He gently pulled back on the control stick and the Fly hovered upward. Walstib lowered it onto his palm, turned it off, then put it away in the container. He put the Fly box in his backpack and pulled out another small box. He aimed one side of the box at the keyhole and pushed a button. A sharp red light shone into the key hole for a second, then switched off. The box hummed almost imperceptibly for a moment then stopped. Walstib opened the box, pulled out a key, and handed it to Ellie.

"Now we have a key."

Yang, barely containing a huge smile, looked at Ellie, "Smallest printer ever."

Ellie was about to put the key in the lock, "What about an alarm?"

"If the laser had detected an alarm, it would have signaled that before it made the key."

"OK, here goes," said Ellie as she turned the key.

The door opened.

CHAPTER 36

They entered the building and continued walking along a corridor. The corridor ended at a closed and unmarked door.

Mae whispered, "I wonder what's in there?"

Walstib whispered, "One way to find out." He opened the door.

Inside the room Walstib saw a large sign that read 'Guards Lounge', three beefy guards wearing AUCO uniforms playing cards, and three guards watching TV. They stopped what they are doing and looked up.

The senior guard gruffly said, "Hey you. What are you doing here?"

In the hall Yang whispered to Ellie, "That's never a good question."

Walstib tried to sound meek, "We're just tourists, and it appears we're lost. Sorry to intrude."

The guard stood up and said, "We?" He walked toward Walstib and pushed him into the hallway so he could take a look at who else was there. "I don't think so," the guard said, even more gruffly.

Yang gave a big smile, "Well you got us there. We're really a rock band scouting out an edgy location for a video shoot."

"Oh how I hate rock 'n roll people. Nothing but trouble. Like right now, you broke in. I'm going to have you arrested."

Ellie leaned in and touched the guard's arm, "You're obviously a smart and observant man and saw through our cover story. We didn't need to break in. We were given a key," she held up the key, "by the Russian government, and asked to perform a surprise inspection."

"Of what?"

Ellie continued, "The nuclear material."

The guard blurted, "That's wrong. The government doesn't know…" He trailed off suddenly realizing his mistake. "I think I need to take you to Mr. Charlie. He runs this place. He'll know what to do with you." He turned and looked back into the guard room, "Hey, a little help here."

Two guards stood up. The senior guard led Walstib, Mae, Ellie, and Yang through the guard room followed by the two additional guards. They were escorted to a large area with an open industrial-type elevator. The senior guard pushed the up button and the elevator, which was parked on the top floor, started down with a loud clang.

CHAPTER 37

The loud clanging noise, louder than the general din of the assembly going on in the facility, caught the attention of Anne and Neil. They turned in the direction of the elevator, looked down, and saw Walstib, Mae, Ellie, and Yang surrounded by the three guards. Two guards had their hands clasped over their guns. The guns were still in their holsters, but the readiness of the guards suggested they weren't part of a welcoming committee.

"This looks bad," whispered Anne.

"I wonder where they're being taken," whispered Neil.

"Look up at the top of the elevator. It lets out on the same level as our catwalk. Let's head over there and find out."

They walked quickly and quietly toward the top of the elevator shaft as the elevator was on its way up.

The elevator reached the top floor and the senior guard, in a gruff voice, said, "This way." One got the impression he was more annoyed at missing his television show than at the possibility of something happening to the facility.

As Walstib and the others were being ushered along by the guards, Neil and Anne fell in behind them.

They arrived at Leake's office, the door, as always, was closed. The senior guard knocked on the door.

"Mr. Charlie, it's Peter Black."

As the guards' attention was focused on the door, Neil gave a subtle tap on Walstib's shoulder. Neil and Anne could just make out the faintest movement of a suppressed smile.

"Come in," said Leake.

Peter Black, the senior guard, walked in first and started to explain why he was bringing these intruders up to Leake's office. The other two guards started to push Mae, Yang, and Ellie into the room.

Walstib took the opportunity to turn his head sideways to where he thought Neil was standing and whispered, "Second canister, point and click, only in an emergency."

"Hey, move along," shouted one of the guards to Walstib. The guards assumed they and their new captives would be leaving soon and no one bothered to close the door. Anne and Neil slid into the room unnoticed.

The room was large. One wall had a row of windows that looked out over the assembly areas and the wall behind Leake's desk had a large banner that read 'Control Room'. Under the banner was a row of ten or more monitors that displayed financials and delivery schedules. Another monitor showed projected orbits around the Earth.

The senior guard, still scowling, said, "Sorry, Sir, but these intruders were trying to give me the run-a-round."

Leake grinned, amused that he, as the tenth richest person in the world had suddenly gained control of the richest person. He said, "No worries, I'd say we have them at a disadvantage."

Walstib said, "Perhaps I can explain," and stepped forward. The senior guard, trying to show he was in control, shouted, "Hold it pal," whipped out his pistol and aimed it squarely at Walstib.

Neil's voice from the back of the room whispered, "Is now an emergency?"

Walstib, his voice sounded a little dry, said "Yes, I think so."

There was a faint click, then a blue arc shot from seemingly empty space and hit the senior guard. Peter Black stood still for a moment, blinking, then slumped over slowly onto the floor, still blinking but otherwise unable to move.

Neil and Anne moved a meter or so over in case the other two guards fired their pistols in the direction of the origin of the blue arc. They needn't have worried, the two guards bolted from the room.

Leake lost his grin, "It appears you have me at a disadvantage."

Walstib straightened to his full height. Slightly taller than Leake, he hoped his greater height and additional age would make Leake continue to feel at a disadvantage and cave in quickly to any demands. Walstib suspected the two guards would be back soon with reinforcements. He took an additional step forward, looked Leake directly in the eyes, and in his deepest voice bellowed, "What the hell are you doing?"

Mae had never seen her father so angry.

Just then Walstib's com-phone rang, and, without skipping a beat, in a calm voice said, "Excuse me."

Leake looked very relieved at the pause in what he assumed would be a lengthy rebuke. He managed a meek, "No problem."

Never taking his eyes off Leake, Walstib reached into his pants pocket and pulled out his com-phone, saw who was calling, and said, "Yes, Sir."

The Brazilian President sounded tired, "Hello Wally. We've finished a preliminary census. We're missing about ninety percent of the Theraphasa Blondi spiders and thousands of acres of rainforest are scorched. We don't know if this will tip them to extinction. They are an important part of our ecosystem. I hope you've made headway in your investigation."

"As a matter of fact, I am standing in front of the man responsible for this calamity."

"Who is it?"

"Charles Leake."

"I know him from the conferences. Put me on speaker."

Walstib took the com-phone from his ear, pushed the speaker button, held the phone out in front of him, and said, "It's the President of Brazil."

Leake's eyes opened wide.

The Brazilian President didn't sound tired now, he sounded very mad, "Leake, what the hell are you doing? We're missing the majority of our spiders and have thousands of acres of scorched trees. I'm authorizing Dr. Walstib to arrest you if you don't fix this problem right now."

Leake continued to look at Walstib, and in a calm deliberate tone, honed from years of business negotiations, stated, "I'll return all the spiders within a month and donate a billion WUs for reforestation."

"Can I trust you or do I put a financial freeze on all your holdings here?"

"You can trust me, Sir."

CHAPTER 38

In the outskirts of Moscow was a small gray building with no windows and very thick walls. The Generals all had to put their palms on an electronic scanner to open the door. After they each were individually admitted into the elevator they went down several floors to a conference room. The conference room had a brass plaque inscribed with the words 'Generals Briefing Room'. The plaque hadn't been polished recently. There were twenty seats, a sign of times past, but only four Generals came into the room today. The room was dimly lit.

All of the Generals were big strong men with an abundance of medals on their uniforms. They stood behind their chairs, their backs ramrod straight. Two on one side of the table, and two on the other side, the head chair remained vacant.

General Quill moved from the back unlit portion of the room and walked slowly to his chair at the head of the table. He was bigger than the others, had more medals on his chest, and a few years earlier might have been labeled as a force to be reckoned with. He looked straight ahead and barked a deep voiced, "Take seats."

The other Generals sat down first, then their commander sat down.

General Quill began slowly, "Gentlemen, good to see you. Thank you for assembling on such short notice." He looked each one in the eyes. "As you know, our battle readiness is not what it should be. Our training budgets have been slashed year after year. We haven't had a good war in two decades." He paused for a moment, looking at the four others, "Unless anyone here has started a little war somewhere for practice?" He raised his eyebrows, waiting for an answer.

The other Generals shook their heads no.

"Well, I didn't think so, but you never know." He paused again, as if someone might actually fess up, then resumed in a quiet voice, "Apparently there is a private group in Russia that is in possession of nuclear material."

The other Generals, shocked, looked at each other then back at their leader.

He continued in a slightly more urgent tone, "This type of clandestine operation can only happen when the world perceives us as weak. There is no telling what they will do with this illegal material." He stabbed a finger at the desk, "We are going to move on this group. And we are going to move with force. If they are rogue terrorists, we will take them out. If they are a rogue company, we have been authorized to shut them down and extract a substantial fine. Enough WUs to bring our battle group back up to full strength and make our countrymen proud of us."

One of the Generals, looking hopeful and rubbing his fingers together, said, "And a little for us?"

General Quill, saddened to realize how deep the budget cuts had hit, looked back at his comrade, and said, "And a little for us."

The other General said, "We're in. When do we assemble the troops?"

Quill stood up, "Right now."

CHAPTER 39

Walstib looked at Leake angrily, "It's much harder to reforest a rainforest than you think."

Leake, used to getting his way was quick to blame others, "Those *dropouts*. They caught the trees on fire? They were supposed to scare the spiders into jumping in the nets with smoke guns, not torches. That just cost me a billion WUs."

"I'm curious, what was your plan?" Walstib asked. He was pretty sure he knew the plan, but asking the architect of a plan directly was always a good idea.

Leake stood up straight, he was proud of his plan, and here was someone with connections right in front of him. Maybe, he thought, he could persuade Dr. Walstib to see his perspective and help should there be any last minute glitches. "Throughout the world, my people work night and day to find new business opportunities. I knew from my mining operations that gold and platinum arrived on Earth via meteor showers over two-hundred million years ago. So, I had my team hack into the U.S. Space Service's Near Earth Object Program to search the composition of anything coming toward Earth. When they found this new asteroid filled with gold I knew I had to have it. I bought Russian rocket ships, fitted them with nuclear engines to speed them up to intercept this asteroid, snare it with spider webbing, direct it back to Earth, park it in orbit, mine the gold, and voila!" he snapped his fingers gleefully, "I pass right by you and become the richest man in the world!" He realized that his bravado might not make Walstib come over to his team, but he didn't care. The thought of being number one was too mesmerizing.

Mae practically snorted, "What could possibly go wrong?"

"Nothing," snapped Leake.

Walstib gestured for Mae to calm down, "Actually, she has a point. I have a few questions about your plan."

"I've thought this through, I think you'll be impressed."

"First, don't you know that it's a comet and not an asteroid?"

"So?"

"A comet is mostly ice. If you try to steer it towards Earth, then try to stop it with a web the ice will break apart. You can't park it."

"Great, the ice goes away and it's easier for us to mine the gold."

"But the amount of ice is massive. If it continues towards Earth it could destroy us like the comet that destroyed the dinosaurs."

"We think it will be burned up in the atmosphere."

"You think so. Secondly, what if you park the gold core too close to Earth and it gets caught in our gravity?"

"We have thousands of kilometers of spider silk for webbing. It should hold."

"And if it doesn't hold?"

"We send up more rockets with more webbing."

Neil leaned close to Yang and whispered, "Fissile said the rocket engines won't work."

Yang cleared his throat and whispered to Walstib, "Fissile said the rocket engines won't work."

Walstib turned his head slightly and flashed a grin, then turned back to Leake, "We hear the rocket engines won't work."

Leake looked furious. He waved his hand toward the door. The two guards who left had returned with another ten guards and had been standing in the doorway waiting for Leake's signal.

They re-entered the room all pointing their pistols at Walstib.

Leake started a hysterical rant, "What do you mean you've heard? Are you working for one of my competitors? Are you here to shut down my project? I don't have time for this." He pointed a finger at Walstib, "It looks like I now have the upper hand. I was going to invite you to work with me, but forget it. Now you're not going to be in contact with anyone. Give me your com-phone."

Walstib handed his com-phone to Leake.

Leake opened it up, took out the chip inside, smashed the chip on the floor, and flung the com-phone back at Walstib. "I know how these things work, I'm not stupid. Now give me that blue arc thing."

Walstib turned his head around slowly and looked at where he thought Neil was standing, "There's too many of them. Let's do as he says. Turn the first canister upside down and push the button again."

Everyone could hear a little click. The canister started to inhale the invisibility material. Neil became visible. He then went through the same procedure for Anne and she became visible.

One of the guards could be heard talking to one of the other guards, "I gotta get me one of them."

Walstib looked at Neil, "Hand me both canisters."

Neil handed him the canisters.

Walstib double clicked the buttons on the invisibility canister and the blue arc canister triggering an internal disabling process rendering them useless and unable to be reverse engineered. He smiled and handed both to Leake. "I think this quest is clouding your judgment."

Leake was still furious, "I have nothing but good judgment. I started with nothing, and every decision I've made has brought me more money. And, I create jobs. You guys getting paid well?" He looked at the guards as if rallying them to his cause.

They all cheered in response.

Leake continued, "Plus, I will be helping the world by providing a rare commodity. The electronics, medical, and jewelry industries all need tonnes of gold. There is a fixed amount of raw materials on Earth, and one of the many things I've learned in business is that people will pay dearly for something that is rare."

Mae had heard enough, "You need more money? Didn't you see the Jimmy Stewart classic 'It's a Wonderful Life'? More isn't always better you know."

Leake now seemed more determined than angry, "I can't have you all around wasting my time with silly questions. And I can't let you go and tell the competition. You all will stay here until I have successfully completed this project."

"But," Walstib protested, "you'll send the spiders back?"

"I've invested billions in this. And I'll make trillions. So I'm not worried about a few spiders. They'll stay here until the project is finished too." Leake turned to the guards. "Take them away."

The guards escorted Walstib, Mae, and the Sci Crew out of the room.

The senior guard, still on the floor, let out a soft groan. He stood up, wobbling, hoisted his pistol in the air, and looked at Leake, "Don't worry boss, I've got this."

CHAPTER 40

The entire contingent of guards, slowly and nervously, escorted their charges down the hall to the other end of the building. They arrived at a door with a small sign that read, 'Guest Quarters'.

The guard in front opened the door and signaled for the captives to go in. The other guards held back, having heard now about the blue arc they were unsure of what other tricks these intruders might have.

The guest room was a small but comfortable area, equipped with two sets of bunk beds, four chairs, a table, and a serviceable kitchenette. It didn't look as if it had been used in years, ever since the last company had rented the facility. Leake obviously didn't have many guests.

The guard said, "We'll bring you some food in a bit." He closed the door. They heard a click in the lock.

Walstib smiled, "So…poaching, arson, theft of nuclear material, hacking a government agency, and now kidnapping. I'd say we have Leake right where we want him."

Mae frowned, "Other than the fact that we are locked in a room with armed guards outside."

"There's that, but not to worry," Walstib smiled and pulled out his com-phone. He texted a message. "The shuttle-bus will be here shortly."

The Sci Crew stared at Walstib's com-phone, then stared at him.

Ellie pointed at the com-phone, "But we saw Leake take the chip out."

"He took *a* chip out, a duplicate chip. The main chip is built into the frame of the com-phone. Didn't you see the old James Bond film 'Goldfinger'?"

They shook their heads no.

"Goldfinger was smuggling gold across the border, the guards kept looking in the trunk but never found any gold. He had made the car itself out of gold. You'll learn that information doesn't just come from school books, it comes from everywhere: books, TV, movies, the Web, museums, lectures, conversations with friends…everywhere. In order to think outside the box, you have to learn outside the box."

Anne smiled and poked at Yang, "So your comic books may come in handy someday."

Walstib smiled to himself, he had been right, this group of four that had literally dropped out of the sky was smart. As smart as his daughter Mae. As smart as Mae's mother.

"Hey, I'm a little tired. I'm going to grab some shuteye. Once we're out of here, we'll shut down this comet thing."

He went over to the first bunk, lay down, and fell asleep a nanosecond after his head hit the pillow.

Neil looked at the others, "Come over to the table. I have a better idea."

CHAPTER 41

A column of twenty of the latest model Russian tank was making good speed as they wound along the narrow roads leading away from Moscow and toward Elektrostal. General Quill's tank was the lead tank, he had his head out of the turret so he could watch the countryside roll by. It was clear treading all the way. He couldn't help but think that this would be the easiest battle he ever fought.

CHAPTER 42

Mae, Anne, Ellie, and Yang sat around the table. Neil stood while he described his initial concept. Ideas, numbers, equations, and possible sources for equipment went flying back and forth among the Sci Crew for fifteen minutes. Anne discussed the possible gravitational effects.

"It sounds good, but I'd like to get to a supercomputer and crunch some numbers," said Yang, looking straight ahead as if he was already constructing some of the calculations in his head.

Ellie discussed the potential biological implications. Sometimes they got too excited and they had to remind themselves that Walstib was sleeping only a few feet away. Finally, Neil asked, "Mae, what do you think?"

"Do you want to know what I think or what I think my dad will think?" Mae asked in a straightforward manner. She was used to only being asked about her father's opinion.

Ellie looked right at Mae, "We want to know what *you* think."

"My dad runs all his ideas past me first. I think just to make sure they aren't too wacky, before he commits time and resources. So I'm used to hearing wacky. This is not wacky. This is brilliant."

Before they could continue, Walstib's com-phone buzzed. He woke up, reached into his pocket, got his com-phone, and looked at the screen. "Mae, could you please toss me my backpack?" It was slung over the back of her chair. She tossed it to her dad and he looked inside. He pulled out a third canister. "They're pretty inept at being bad guys," smiled Walstib, "they were in such a hurry they didn't even take our stuff." He walked to the center of the room, held out his com-phone, pushed a button, then jumped back a few steps. A second or two later, there was a kind of dull thwap sound as a steel arrow pierced the cement roof. Two toggle barbs sprang out and the cable pulled upward securing the mechanism to the roof. Walstib gestured to everyone to move back as he again moved to the center of the room. He took his new canister, pointed it at the ceiling, and clicked the button. A powerful laser beam shot out and he carved a large circle about three meters in diameter on the ceiling. He pushed another button on his com-phone and the mechanism lowered the round roof section soundlessly to the floor. Walstib unhooked the arrow mechanism from the cable, pushed another button and the cable pulled back up. A few seconds later a large steel rescue cage lowered into the room through the hole in the roof.

Walstib pointed to the cage and said, "Hop in."

As everyone was stepping into the cage they heard the door unlock.

"Hurry," Walstib whispered.

The senior guard came in with a tray of food. He looked right at them, and his smile turned into a look of surprise.

"If we don't move maybe he won't see us," said Anne in a voice loud enough for the guard to hear. She hoped it would make him less angry. She smiled at him.

The guard smiled back, put the tray on the table, turned to Walstib and said, "Take me with you."

Walstib looked him in the eyes, and said in a very serious tone, "Will you testify against Leake?"

"Yes," said the guard without hesitation. "While I was on the floor, I heard your whole conversation. Leake's maniacal. He won't mind getting us all killed as long as he makes money."

"Climb on in," said Walstib as he held the cage door open.

CHAPTER 43

The senior guard, although at this point he realized Leake would no longer consider him the senior guard, climbed into the rescue cage, and Walstib pushed a button on his com-phone. The cage was pulled up through the roof and into the open bay at the back of the hovering Shuttle Bus. The bay doors closed and everyone climbed out of the cage.

Walstib made for the pilot's seat and sat down. He looked forward for a moment, stood up, and said, "First things first, we have to take care of Leake. Mae, you drive. Switch to manual." He looked at the guard, "Peter, do you know where the local police station is?"

Peter Black nodded yes, shocked at being treated pleasantly.

"All right, you give Mae directions."

Mae jumped into the pilot's seat and Black slid into the navigator's seat and started pointing the way.

The Sci Crew sat in the back seats.

Walstib, standing, still clutching his com-phone dialed the Russian President. "Hi, Walstib again. President Tereshkova please."

"Yes, Sir," the aide quickly responded.

After a brief moment, the president came on the line, "Wally, I was about to call you. There has been an unusually large flow of WUs, apparently billions, being transferred from AUCO's U.S. bank into their Brazilian and Russian banks. These are vast sums and they will probably fight to protect their investment. You have to be careful."

"We will, thank you. Let me fill you in on what we've found. AUCO has kept the nuclear material they were supposed to deliver to your storage facilities. Madam President, please notify the police station in Elektrostal and tell them to arrest Leake. We'll go there and fill them in on the details."

"I'll do that right now."

"Secondly, I would advise that you freeze the financial assets of AUCO and any other holdings belonging to Charles Leake."

"Will do. Is that it?"

"That's it for now, I'll call later and fill you in."

"There's one more thing from my end," said Tereshkova. "Now that I know you're there and Leake has nuclear material at his site, this next piece of information is vitally important. It appears that someone on my staff has leaked the AUCO financials to someone in the military. One of our top generals, without my authorization, is leading twenty tanks to Leake's site. If it was just a financial matter, he would know it was a police matter. However, I now assume he also knows about the nuclear material which is why he jumped into action."

"This isn't a terrorist operation. Can you get your general to stand down? I'd hate for this to escalate and compromise the nuclear material."

"Wait one."

Walstib could hear Tereshkova telling an aide to try to reach the General.

There was a brief pause.

Tereshkova came back on the line, "We can't get through. I suppose they are in attack mode and have switched to communications blackout."

"How far out are they from Leake's site?"

"About one hour."

Walstib paused, "An hour…that's cutting it close. If you can call the police station…I'll take care of the military."

CHAPTER 44

Walstib made a call to his lab, "Juice up the HyperRider, load it with 100 Sticky Bots, set the drop over Elektrostal Russia, set the bots for heat seek and perimeter containment pattern, and launch immediately. Thanks." He hung up.

Neil was about to speak, but Walstib held up a finger to indicate one more minute.

Walstib called the President of Brazil, "A quick update, Sir. Leake has no intention of returning the spiders. I'll work to see that it happens, but I'm afraid you'll need to freeze his assets to take care of the reforestation."

"We'll take care of the finance on this end. Call me later to arrange for shipment of the spiders. Thanks Wally"

They hung up.

Neil again tried to speak.

Walstib was already making another call, to Wolfred Dire, the President of the United States. "Dr. Walstib for President Dire, please."

The President's assistant patched Walstib through without saying a word. Walstib felt that when aides only said "We'll put you through" it sounded perfunctory, however, when they said nothing it sounded cold and distant. He wasn't sure which he liked least.

The President came on the line, "Wally? Is that you? I can barely hear you, sorry, I've got a deca of aides and corporate executives in here yammering about something. I think the rubber manufacturers are trying to make it mandatory that all cars be made of rubber in order to cut down on accidents. I think the idea has some merit."

And their idea has nothing to do with the campaign funds they gave you to gain access or the potential windfall profits the industry stands to gain, thought Walstib. He decided against bringing up that topic. "Perhaps it merits a study. But right now Mr. President I'm calling on an urgent matter. We request that you freeze all the assets of Charles Leake's companies."

"What's this all about?"

"It would be helpful if we could discuss this later."

"Wally, tell me something."

Walstib hesitated, "Trying to diffuse a situation with the Russian army and a stockpile of nuclear material. I'll call you later. In the meantime, *please* do not tell anyone else about this."

"OK. OK. We'll freeze the assets. Call me later." The President hung up.

Walstib looked at the Sci Crew, "I really don't like giving information to politicians. They have a way of mucking things up. Now what were you trying to tell me?"

Neil started to talk but was cut off by Mae.

"We're landing at the police station."

Mae landed the Shuttle Bus smoothly.

Walstib smiled and gave a little head nod at Mae letting her know she had done a good job of flying and landing the Shuttle Bus. "Mae, why don't you take Peter into the police station. Hopefully President Tereshkova has called by now. And let them know twenty tanks will be arriving. The tanks won't be able to negotiate through the streets in front so they will likely show up in the field in the back of Leake's facility. Leake's guards, when faced with a fight or flee decision, will probably flee out the front door and the police should wait for them there rather than trying to fight their way in. We'll take care of the tanks."

Mae looked at Peter and said, "Come on Mr. Black. *Let's move out.*" She winked at her dad.

CHAPTER 45

President Dire sat behind his desk in the Oval Office. He
stared at his phone. Did he just hear that right? he
wondered. "Everyone out of the room," he said in a soft
voice, as if he was still thinking about what he had just
heard.

The aides and corporate executives looked at him.

"Let's do a study. Department of Transportation will pay
for it. Now please everyone, out."

Everyone left the room.

The President stared at the electronic picture frame on his
desk. The picture was of George Washington. "Nope," He
said. He pushed the button on the frame and a picture of
Abraham Lincoln came on the screen. "Nope," he said
again. He pushed the button again. His picture came on the
screen, a big smarmy politico grin on his face with the
American flag behind him. "Now there's a leader. What
should I do?" he asked himself aloud. "Walstib said not to
tell anyone. But the Russian army? Nuclear material? US
citizens? US corporate interests? This could be a major
threat. And I'm obligated under international treaty to bring
this to the attention of the U.N."

The President composed himself, and pushed a button on
his desk com-phone, "Secretary General of the United
Nations."

The Secretary General of the United Nations spoke into her
com-phone, "Hello, Mr. President, good to hear from you."

"Protocol dictates that I notify you if I become aware of
any potential international incident. There is something
happening now between the Russian Army and U.S.

personal. The person who told me this had to break off, perhaps he was being attacked. I don't know anything more than that. So, for the time being, let's keep this just between us."

"Of course, Mr. President. Not a word. Thank you for alerting me." They hung up. She pushed a button on her desk com-phone and called to her assistant, "Can you come in right now, please." It wasn't a question, not in that tone. Her assistant came into her office.

The Secretary General was still in mid-thought and didn't realize she hadn't brought her assistant up to speed on the conversation with the President. "Not a word, my foot," she said. "That's how problems arose between squabbling countries. Lies. Backstabbing. It always starts small but quickly escalates. People are dying and he wants secrecy? Full disclosure is what is needed. Play it out in full view of the world. Both sides will be embarrassed and back down. I'll fix this." She looked directly at her assistant, "Call all the delegates, we need a full U.N. assembly."

CHAPTER 46

Mae and Peter Black were welcomed into the Elektrostal police station with open arms. They sat around a table and had croissants, strawberries, and hot tea while the Captain of the police station took great delight in describing how he had personally taken the call from President Tereshkova. The other members of the police force didn't pay much attention to their Captain as they surreptitiously peeked out the front window at the other-worldly looking Shuttle Bus parked in the front parking lot.

Mae described the overall plan and Black described the location details: the streets, the door in the front of the facility, the fence, and the loading dock.

The Captain nodded and agreed to the plan. The Captain had spent most of this time looking raptly at Mae, however, when he looked at the uniform Peter Black was wearing, he asked, "Isn't he one of them?"

Black looked a little nervous.

Mae stood up, "He's with us. He was undercover."

The Captain stood up, "I can't help but think I've seen him before. Anyway, we'll take it from here. We appreciate the opportunity to serve. I've got to assemble my officers and get a few detention wagons ready. We'll get going soon. Best if you civilians stay clear. I'll bet you wouldn't know what to do if a gun was pointed at you."

Peter Black stood up, and as they headed for the door whispered to Mae, "I'll bet you would."

CHAPTER 47

The HyperRider had been loaded as requested and streaked toward Elektrostal, Russia.

The tanks had turned off the highway in order to approach Leake's facility from the fields behind the facility rather than try to negotiate through the narrow roads in the industrial park.

The Elektrostal police force, all three shifts, which numbered a total of twelve officers, had been assembled and each drove a car or detention wagon to make their ranks appear bigger. They raced toward the industrial park as fast as their old detention wagons could go.

Inside the U.N. Building, in the main Assembly Hall, the 200 or so delegates who represented each country had gathered.

The Secretary General, Joan Casey, believed in her cause. She had been a career bureaucrat her whole life, moving up the administrative ranks without ever having had a real job. And, as did all career politicians, she had a skewed view of the world. She stood at the podium in front, and spoke sternly, "Delegates, I come before you to let you know that Russia and the United States are now at war. The business leaders, military leaders, and scientists have failed us again. Only we highly skilled diplomats can save the day. We must enact a resolution that prohibits all misunderstandings. We must work on this tirelessly until we work out a solution. I ask that you start discussing this

immediately, and hold these discussions in the strictest confidence. There must be no outside distractions. No word of this must leak out until this important and groundbreaking legislation is complete."
The delegates all nodded yes. However, they assumed they were being given another sugar-coated version and assumed the worst. They immediately opened their com-phones and texted, "World at war" to their governments back home.

CHAPTER 48

As the tanks entered the field one by one, they split off and lined up next to each other, rolling forward slowly. They continued to move forward until they came to the base of a small rise, then they came to a stop, engines idling. They were hidden from view by anyone in Leake's facility. "Perfect concealment, no one can see us," General Quill said to the men in his tank. "Pass me the bullhorn." He took the bullhorn, climbed out of his tank, and strutted up the embankment to the top of the slight ridge. Once he reached the top, he barked into his bullhorn, "Charles Leake…come out…surrender or be fired upon." He waited a minute, then repeated his demand.

The ridge was about one hundred meters from the back of the facility, but the bullhorn was loud and could be clearly heard even from that distance.

A figure appeared in a window on the top floor of the building. Inside the facility, Leake stood at the window, pulled out his com-phone, and pushed a couple of buttons to activate the building's intercom system. He spoke into the com-phone, "All guards report outside the back door, weapons drawn. We have what looks like a kook or a terrorist making demands."

On the first level, most of the guards, sensing their first real call to action were excited, unholstered their pistols and ran to the back door.

Two guards, who had been friends for years, looked at each other. The first said, "I didn't sign on to go up against terrorists."

The other said, "Yeah. I thought this was going to be a cozy night-watchman job."

"Let's get out of here."

While the rest of the guards ran toward the back door, the two who had a sudden change of heart ran through the assembly room toward the stairs leading to the downstairs parking garage.

All the assembly workers asked each other what was going on and looked in the direction of the guards running to the back.

The two guards running to the garage saw no one was paying attention to the stockpiles of expensive parts. One said, "Grab something. If Mr. Charlie was going to send us into harm's way, he owes us."

"Yeah," said the other. "We can sell this stuff and make our own fortune."

They grabbed as many parts as they could carry and fled down the stairs toward the garage. They jumped into their car and raced out of the building.

CHAPTER 49

Inside the Shuttle Bus, Anne, Ellie, Neil, and Yang discussed the new Sci Crew plan with Walstib. As they heard the police station door open and close, Walstib motioned to the Shuttle Bus door and said quietly, "Your concept is really, really amazing. Let's hold off on this discussion for the moment."

Mae and Peter walked out of the police station to the Shuttle Bus. Peter climbed in first, then Mae, who closed the door and beamed, "All set."

Walstib smiled, "Well done." He then turned to Peter, "So, Mr. Black, where can we…" Before Walstib finished his sentence, he was interrupted by beeping on his com-phone. He pulled the com-phone from his pocket and read the message aloud, "Sticky Bots dropped." He looked at Peter, "Sorry, we'll drop you off later. We need to observe the Sticky Bots to make sure this all works out."

Walstib climbed into the pilot's seat, Mae sat in the navigator's seat and the others sat in the back. He pushed a few buttons, they lifted off, and he steered toward Leake's facility. Everyone was silent in anticipation. Once they were near AUCO they saw the police cars arriving and one car speeding away.

Peter looked out the side window and commented, "Hey, I know that car. Those guys left before their shift was over. They're going to get a reprimand."

Walstib hovered up higher to get a better look.

Leake barged out of the back door followed by twenty guards. They lined up against the back wall with pistols pointed at the figure on the hill.

General Quill lifted his bullhorn and commanded, "Drop your weapons."

Leake turned back to his guards, "This guy is an idiot. Let's scare him off. Aim high. Fire on three." He turned to face the lone man on the ridge, "One …two…three…fire."' All twenty pistols fired at once, the sound made louder by reverberations off the back wall.

General Quill didn't flinch one bit. He spoke into his com-phone to the tank commanders, "Forward slowly, stop at the top of the ridge."

The row of tanks clanked up the short incline and came to a stop, all barrels aimed at the facility. It was a daunting sight.

The AUCO guards froze in place.

General Quill climbed up on his tank and looked down into the turret, "Load one blank shell. Aim high."

Inside the tank the men moved quickly. The shell was loaded and the barrel moved upward slightly.

He had just been fired upon and Quill wanted the opposing force to know this was personal. He put down the bullhorn and relied on his deep, battle-hardened voice, "Fire."

Leake and his guards heard the command for a split second before a massive wall of sound almost knocked them off their feet.

The barrel lowered and pointed, like the rest of the tanks, directly at the guards.

Leake and the guards pulled at each other to get back through the door. As they ran through the assembly area,

the assembly workers stared at their boss in total disarray.
The workers put down their work in disbelief. A minute
later Leake and the guards tumbled out of the front door
and were met by the small contingent of police officers,
police cars, and police wagons.

Leake and his guards were promptly hauled off to the
Elektrostal jail.

Yang, who had been scanning the sky, pointed and said,
"Up there, here they come."

They all looked up as one hundred Sticky Bots, same
design as the Fire Bots but gleaming silver and hard to spot,
streaked down to Earth homing in on the immense heat
generated by the large tank engines. Once the Sticky Bots
got to a pre-set height above the ground, they banked and
circled the tanks. The bots then released a wide spray of
specially formulated aerogel, which looked like a mixture
of ballistic gel and silly string. Once the aerogel mixture hit
the ground it expanded exponentially faster than the
expanding foam insulation made for the housing market.
The tanks were completely encircled.

General Quill had been amused for a minute thinking this
was a peacenik prank, but had grown concerned when the
bots kept circling.

The wall of Aerogel grew to over ten meters in height and
about ten meters in thickness at the base. Once the bots'
payload was spent they headed back up to rendezvous with
the HyperRider. Now the General was furious. Quill looked
down into the tank and ordered, "Load." They did so. Then
he commanded, "Fire." The tank belched fire, smoke, and a
thunderous boom. The shot went all of two meters into the

gel. "Forward." The tank proceeded but stopped when it became lodged in the gel. The General's next single word was muffled by the wall of gel.

Walstib exhaled.
Mae, Peter, and the Sci Crew whooped and applauded.
Walstib pulled out his com-phone and the applause ebbed.
"Walstib calling for President Tereshkova, please."
By now the calls to the President of Russia were getting routine and everyone else continued to look out the window, or carry on quiet conversations.
"Hello Wally. What's the update?"
"We've captured your rogue tank squadron, in a manner of speaking."
"Where are they?"
"In Elektrostal. They are surrounded by my own blend of aerogel. They aren't going anywhere."
"I'll send several tank squadrons to pick them up. How do we get through the gel?"
"It's biodegradable in water. You can either wait for the first rain or send a few fire trucks along with the tanks."
"I'll have to think about that. It's not supposed to rain for another few days, maybe I should let them stew a while…Hold on." A pause. "I'm being told by my aides that I shouldn't do that." Walstib could hear Tereshkova say to her aides, "All right, send some tanks and a couple of fire trucks to go pick-up Quill and his troops."
"Another thing, please."
"Yes Wally. I am very grateful for your help. Anything you want."

"I'd like to continue making lease payments on the facility here and continue to employ all of Leake's employees. But I need to use the nuclear material for an experiment." He looked at the Sci Crew. "We'll dispose of it for you at no cost."

"That I don't have to think about. Deal. It's all yours. Keep me up to date."

They hung up.

Peter looked at Walstib, "All the employees?"

Walstib smiled back, "All the employees."

"Thank you."

"Where can we drop you?"

"Actually here is just fine. My car is in the basement garage."

"That's perfect. We'll drop you here." Walstib started to lower the Shuttle Bus. "Your first duty is to go into the assembly areas and tell the assembly workers to take the rest of the day off but to report back to work tomorrow."

CHAPTER 50

The Shuttle Bus landed, Peter shook Walstib's hand and said, "Thanks for the second chance. This reminds me of an old saying, 'A broken chain that has been repaired is better than an unbroken chain.' "

Walstib nodded and replied, "See you tomorrow."

Peter waved to the others, jumped out, and ran straight for the Leake facility. Or, he thought, whatever else it might be renamed tomorrow.

Yang wondered aloud to the group, "Is a repaired chain actually better?"

Ellie looked at Yang, "I think he was speaking metaphorically. Don't be so literal."

Walstib turned to the others, "We need to find a place to sleep and wash up."

Mae suggested, "Let's go back to the diner for a quick bite to eat. They'll probably have a good recommendation for a hotel."

"I'm starving," said Anne.

"Me too," said Neil.

"Good suggestion. Here we go," said Walstib. They lifted off and headed to the diner.

Mae looked at the Sci Crew with big, inquisitive eyes, "So, I heard my dad say something was amazing. Did you guys tell him your plan?"

Neil was about to speak, when Walstib broke in, "Hold on just a second." He pulled out his com-phone, and spoke into it, "Contact Dr. Fissile."

A few seconds later, Fissile answered, "Wally?"

"Yes, it's me again. We have a wild plan…an amazing plan…a wildly amazing plan, and would like to discuss it with you. Can you meet us for dinner?"

"Let me check. Oh, wait, I don't have a nuclear plant or nuclear material to oversee anymore. So I'd say I'm free for dinner. I'd be delighted to discuss your plan. Where shall we meet?"

"We're heading to the Good Chow Diner outside your plant."

"Good place. I'll meet you all there."

Walstib turned back to the others, "You know we have to get your plan right the first time. There is no room for error. We don't get thirty-nine prototypes."

CHAPTER 61

The Shuttle Bus hovered to a landing in the diner parking lot. They entered the diner and were greeted like old friends by the same server as before. "Hello, hello. Welcome back. How's the tour going?" she asked.

"Tour?" blanched Walstib.

"I remember you said you were tourists. Seen anything unusual?"

Walstib looked at the others.

They all shook their heads no.

"No, just the beautiful countryside."

"It's pretty boring around here. We don't get many tourists. But we're glad you're here." She guided them to their same booth, and handed them menus, "I'll be right back with your water."

As the server walked away, Mae said, "I'm having the same as before."

Ellie nodded, "Same here. That was delicious."

Everyone else nodded and put their menus down,

Yang looked at Neil and said, "Photovoltaics."

Neil looked back and said, "Wind energy."

Anne said, "Telegraph."

Ellie said, "Ball bearings."

They looked at Mae.

Mae raised her eyebrows and looked back.

Ellie said, "Don't you play BIDE?"

"What's BIDE?"

"I'm so sorry, we just thought…" She looked at the other Sci Crew members then back at Mae. "It's Best Invention or Discovery Ever."

Yang added, "We play whenever we have a little downtime. You know, we're *biding* our time."

Nobody laughed.

"I liked it," protested Yang.

Neil commented, "The first person says an invention or discovery. Then the next person has their turn. It can't be anything named from the last games. So, for example, we can't use the wheel, movable type, the telephone, the personal computer, or LEDs in this round."

Ellie continued, "Then we debate as to which one had the most influence on society. Whoever's input wins gets a point. So far it's pretty even."

Mae smiled, "Well then, Tupperware."

Anne looked at Neil, Yang, and Ellie, "Wow. A low tech curveball. Gram for gram, I'd say that's a winner."

Walstib leaned over and said "I vote for photovoltaics."

Mae looked at him, "Dad, you can't own the world's biggest solar company and vote for your own invention." She looked at the Sci Crew, "Can he vote like that?"

Neil said calmly, "He can. But I'm voting for your answer."

Yang agreed, "Tupperware it is."

Ellie looked at Walstib, "Sorry Wally, it's five to one."

Fissile walked in the front door, waved at the waitress, looked around, and came over to the table. "Hello everyone. Good to see you again. Wally you look glum."

"Welcome, sit down. I am glum. For the second time in an hour I've been bested by the next generation."

The server came over and they ordered their food.

Walstib continued, "First these guys think of a plan that I didn't even consider and now Tupperware beats photovoltaics in their game of influential inventions."
Fissile smiled at Walstib, "Tupperware was ubiquitous well before photovoltaics, and probably every home in the world has Tupperware. So smile-up dude and tell me about this plan."
Everyone laughed.

The food arrived and they all discussed the plan in detail over their delicious meal.

After the discussion ended and the plates were cleared away, Walstib asked Fissile, "Well, what do you think?"
"I can get the nuclear rockets to work but I'm concerned about the spider webbing."
Walstib pulled out his com-phone, "Let me call a spider expert that I know." He spoke into the com-phone, "Contact Dr. Pod, please."

Dr. Arthur Pod, the world's leading specialist in spider webs and spider DNA was in his laboratory. Much like police dogs had been trained to attack aggressors, Pod was testing spiders to see if they could be trained to crawl under doors and spray webbing onto perpetrators to subdue them. This would avoid all the hazards of breaking a door down with an unknown hostile lurking behind the door.
Pod answered his com-phone, "Hey Wally, long time."
"Hey Art, sorry I have to be quick. Do you have a minute?"
"Of course."

"I have a few colleagues with me. May I put you on speaker?"

"All right."

"If we wanted to capture something in space, do you think it's possible to use spider webbing?"

"Like space debris?"

"Like that, but bigger and with more mass."

"Everyone's been trying to make a synthetic web formula for a variety of uses, including uses in ultra cold environments. We still have a long way to go in the DNA process. If the item was small with relatively less mass, I'd say regular spider webbing would hold up. However, with a larger more massive item you should fortify the webbing with flexible nano-tubing."

"Like the flexible steel mesh surrounding rubber tubing for uses in plumbing?" asked Fissile.

"Exactly," said Pod.

Walstib nodded at Fissile, "We can do that."

Pod continued, "However, if you capture something and bring it to Earth, I'd be more concerned with the potential problems resulting from bringing new biological organisms from a foreign body into contact with life on Earth. Life on Earth may have been started by life forms arriving from comets or asteroids billions of years ago, but newly arriving organisms may not be compatible with us today. Because of that concern, the original astronauts returning from the moon were decontaminated and quarantined for days."

"Good point. We'll be aware of the potential for biological contamination. I think we can work on that," Walstib said pointing at Mae and the Sci Crew.

They nodded excitedly.

"Thanks buddy, I'll fill you in later." They hung up.

Walstib looked at Fissile, "It looks like we can accommodate the spider webbing issue. Is that enough for you?"

"This is an amazing plan. I'm in….but, I have to say I'm a bit disappointed."

Everyone looked shocked.

"I thought we were going to make a rock video."

Mae smiled at Fissile, "Perhaps we will someday."

They had finished their meal and Walstib signaled for the bill.

The server brought over the check. As Walstib put his fingerprint on the billing tablet, he asked, "Is there a nice hotel nearby?"

Before the server could answer, Fissile interrupted, "No need. You can all stay with me. I have government supplied housing as part of my compensation package, I think it can accommodate all of you."

Everyone looked a little skeptical.

"I think you'll find it cozy. I insist."

"Are you sure you won't mind us? It may be a while."

"No bother at all, I'd appreciate the company. It's not far. I'll drive home, you follow me."

Walstib looked at the server, "Looks like we'll be staying in the area for a while to do some more sightseeing. I expect we'll be seeing you again."

"Then I should introduce you," said Fissile. "This is Wally, Mae, Anne, Ellie, Neil, and Yang. And our server is Donna and her husband, the chef, is Keith."

Donna smiled, "You can tell us apart. He's the wild looking guy with the chef's apron and I'm the pretty one."

"I heard that," came from Keith in the kitchen.

CHAPTER 62

The two guards who had bolted at the Leake facility sat on their worn sofa in their small apartment. They had changed out of their guard uniforms and into jeans and t-shirts. They stared at the pile of objects on the coffee table, the items they had stolen on their way out of the facility.

The first guard stared vacantly and asked, "What did we get?"

The second guard, looked quizzical and responded, "I don't know. I don't even know what they were building at the warehouse."

"But it's high-tech stuff right?"

"I hope so. Someone will pay something for it. I'll make some calls."

President Dire sat alone at his desk in the Oval Office staring at a bank of com-screens. One screen showed financial news, another international news, another a live feed of The Senate debates, and another, the one with the sound up, was The TMX Network, their tagline: 'Extreme Celebrities – All the Time'. The reporter gushed about the beautiful starlet who had finished her rehab at Mother McCree's Rehab Center and had gone out on the street to hug her well-wishers. "She's so brave. Each time she comes out of rehab she can talk so openly with anyone she meets." The reporter was interrupted by another reporter, "We bring you this exclusive news. Our sources at the U.N. tell us that the world is going to war. We'll send in our crack team of reporters and let you know what the U.N. delegates were wearing when they learned of this news.

Back to our regularly scheduled programming." The President said to himself, "Walstib says 'Nothing to worry about.' What does he know?" He muted the com-screen and buzzed his assistant. "Call the Joint Chefs and ask if we're at war. And send some more flowers to Mother McCree's."

The assistant buzzed back, "I heard she was out."

"She'll be back in by the time the flowers arrive."

CHAPTER 53

Fissile pulled into a long driveway. He drove slowly, and the Shuttle Bus followed slowly.

Yang ventured, "This thing won't stall, will it?"

Walstib looked back, "We can accommodate any speed that Fissile feels comfortable driving."

"Oh, my goodness," interrupted Mae. "I was expecting a cramped guest cottage."

Fissile came to a stop and the Shuttle Bus landed a few meters away.

Fissile jumped out of his car and greeted his guests as they climbed down from the Shuttle Bus.

"Welcome to my humble abode."

They looked up at what could easily be a thirty-room dacha.

"This is a hold-over from the era of the tsars," Fissile explained. "The government owns and maintains it as a historical landmark. It's the closest house to the nuclear plant, so they let me use it. I've been the sole lodger for years. Please, come in."

They walked inside and everyone was agape at the grandeur. The beauty of the craftsmanship in the wood beams and paneling was unparalleled in today's modern homes.

Fissile gestured upstairs, "Guest bedrooms are upstairs. Pick any one you want. Each room has its own bathroom."

"Get a good night's sleep," added Walstib. "We've got a lot of work to start tomorrow. You might want to call your parents. Tell them you've seen some beautiful countryside, but I wouldn't mention your plan."

Mae and the Sci Crew bounded upstairs.

"Let's go into the drawing room. I've got some ideas as to where we can source the nano-tubing," said Fissile. "Care for some rare brandy while we talk?"

"I'd love some," replied Walstib.

"Good."

As they walked to the drawing room, Walstib looked at Fissile, "Smile-up dude?"

"Hey, it's a line from a new song I really like."

CHAPTER 54

Walstib, Mae, and the Sci Crew came downstairs to find
Fissile standing in the kitchen.

Fissile exclaimed, "Good morning! I've got coffee, tea,
milk, and homemade doughnuts waiting for you."

Yang and Neil each grabbed a doughnut, took a bite, and
gave grunts of thanks to Fissile. Mae, Ellie, and Anne gave
Fissile a group hug and then sat down and each poured a
cup of tea.

"This is fabulous, thank you," said Walstib, as he poured a
cup of coffee.

"Down the hall," said Fissile as he pointed, "is a laundry
room and some old nuclear plant uniforms. They're all
clean. As each shift departed for the last time, I collected
their uniforms and stored them here. You can pick one that
fits and wear them while your laundry is being done."

Yang and Neil, both still chewing a second doughnut said,
"We're OK."

Anne looked at Yang and Neil and scrunched her nose, "As
he said, the laundry room is down the hall."

Ellie nodded and pointed down the hall.

Walstib put down his coffee, "I'll go first." He walked
down the hall and came back wearing a faded yellow
jumpsuit. "Last one push the start button."

One by one they went down the hall and changed.

"Well that does feel better," said Neil. He looked at Fissile,
"Thanks."

Mae looked at Fissile, "There are a lot of uniforms back
there. How many would you say you have?"

"Oh…. three hundred and twelve. Roughly. Why?"

Mae looked at her dad, "You don't want all your new employees wearing AUCO uniforms do you?"

"New employees?...We're late." Walstib looked at Fissile, "The uniform idea makes sense. OK with you?"

"We don't need them here anymore. Feel free."

"Quick, everyone grab as many uniforms as you can, throw on your shoes, and let's get going."

Neil and Yang each grabbed another doughnut and followed the others to the laundry room. They all ran out to the Shuttle Bus, each clutching a huge pile of uniforms, and filed on board. Walstib took off at top speed.

The Shuttle Bus landed in the front of the assembly facility. They clambered out awkwardly with all the uniforms and were met at the front door by Peter Black.

"Glad to see you've found the correct entrance," Peter smiled as he held the door open. "I've talked with the entire assembly staff and they are delighted to have you as their new boss. They are all waiting for you in the rocket assembly area."

"Thank you, Peter," said Walstib. Everyone gave Peter a smile as they went into the building.

Walstib, Fissile, Mae, Anne, Ellie, Neil, and Yang walked into the rocket assemble room and were greeted by loud applause. As they walked by individual workers, each dressed in their own clothes, they passed out the yellow uniforms.

Walstib stepped up on an assembly table and looked out at about one hundred assembly personnel. He held up his hands and gestured for the room to get quiet. "Thank you. In the past you were all selected for the quality of your work and I am very happy that you elected to stay on. As you know there has been a change in management." More applause. "The last manager had as his goal, expansion of his own already vast wealth. Our goal, and when I say 'our', I am referring to my colleagues, Mae, Anne, Neil, Ellie, and Yang for coming up with the concept." More applause as Mae and the Sci Crew beamed. Mae whispered to Ellie, "I've never been called a colleague before."

Walstib continued, "Our goal is to make this corner of the universe a better place. We will also make your pocketbooks a little better as we will share the profits with our workers."

Applause, hoots, and whistles broke out from the assembly workers.

"We have a small window of opportunity here. We need to catch the comet in its orbit as it comes this way. If we delay, and it goes past us, it will be impossible to catch it and bring it back. Its orbit only brings it this close to Earth once every 10,000 years. We'll need to install the extra material and re-build the rocket engines quickly. We ask that you work fast, but the most important thing is one hundred percent accuracy. We only have one shot at this. There is no room for error."

A voice rang out from the back of the room, "If we're not AUCO any more, what are we called?"

Walstib drew a blank, and looked over at the Sci Crew. They huddled for a moment, then Mae whispered to her dad.

Walstib nodded and looked back at the crowd, "Phase Two Enterprises. Now, everyone put on your new uniforms. Dr. Fissile will work with the rocket assembly team to redesign the engines and I will get with the spider webbing team to design a new device to spool nano-tubing onto the silk." He looked out over the excited workers and clapped his hands in appreciation of them.

As he climbed down from the assembly table, there was cheering from the crowd as they chanted in unison, "Phase Two. Phase Two. Phase Two."

CHAPTER 55

Four days later, hundreds of large plastic drums labeled 'Carbon Nano-Tubing' had been delivered and were neatly stacked at one end of the web assembly room. Walstib, Ellie, Yang, and Mae went over the final design for the device that would spool the silk and the nano-tubing together. The assembly workers listened intently to the discussion.

The amount of webbing needed to hold the ice in the comet together had been discussed earlier. They were certain not enough webbing had been created. Adding aerogel to the mix had been considered, but it was determined that adding the gel on Earth would make it too bulky to launch, and adding it in space, where oxygen was needed as a catalyst, would be problematic. Thus, the spiders worked overtime to create additional webbing. A laboratory had been contacted to supply copious amounts of flies, and the spiders were being fed like royalty. There was no real way to know, but as the amount of webbing had increased over previous levels, they were pretty certain the spiders were happy to contribute.

The rocket assembly personnel worked to disassemble the old configuration of the nuclear rockets while Fissile, Anne, and Neil worked out the bugs in the new design. Everyone understood the need to work hard to make up for the lost time caused by the faulty original designs. The assembly teams agreed to work during their lunch breaks and Walstib provided free lunches catered by Donna and Keith.

CHAPTER 56

The two former guards waited anxiously in their apartment. Their calls had mostly been met with negative responses. However, one person seemed interested. He was expected any minute now. The two didn't talk, but each speculated at the riches they would soon have bestowed upon them. Despite the fact that there was a door bell, there was a knock on the door, a loud intense knock that meant 'we have arrived, respond now'. The two guards looked at each other with anticipation. They had speculated that the person coming would be a scientist or engineer, and most probably would be meek and cave in to their demands for a high payment. They opened their apartment door and three large men walked in abruptly. Two of the men grabbed the two guards and held them down in their chairs. The third pulled out a small, extremely sensitive Geiger counter and waved it over the items on the table. The clicks were miniscule, trace amounts that would not affect humans, but they were there.

"Where did you get these?" demanded the man with the Geiger counter.

Fearing these were police officials, the first guard meekly murmured, "That stuff is ours. We've always had it."

The man pulled out a gun and pointed it at the guard, "It's not yours. And we don't want it. But your description of it could only indicate that it was meant to hold nukers. We want the nukers."

Nukers was slang for nuclear materials. These weren't cops. These men were after nuclear material. People like this usually killed for what they wanted.

"OK. OK. This stuff came from the Leake facility in the old warehouse district."

"What's the security like?"

"There's no security. All the guards were arrested a few days ago."

"We heard about that."

"See? We're telling the truth. The information we've given you has got to be worth something."

"How about we spare your life. Is that enough?"

CHAPTER 57

Walstib, Fissile, Mae, and the Sci Crew discussed their progress over lunch.

Yang commented, "I think the nano-tubing spooling device is complete."

Walstib nodded, "I agree, it's ready to go."

Anne looked at Neil, "Dr. Fissile's changes on the rocket engine design look good."

Fissile looked up from his food, "Thank you. I think everything is looking good too. However, for something this key to the project I think we need a test run."

"I don't want to use up one of the rockets, in case of a failure. It would take up a lot of time to find and procure another one," winced Walstib.

"Can we test an engine by hooking one up to the HyperRider?" suggested Neil.

"Do you know how much that scramjet costs? I'll bet 50 times what a rocket shell costs," blurted Ellie.

"Probably more," said Walstib softly. "But we are running out of time. Worst case scenario, I can always build another HyperRider at another time."

"You're testing it on autopilot, I assume?" asked Mae.

Walstib looked at Fissile, "Probably not. I would have to pilot it to get a feel for any anomalies and make corrections."

Mae held her dad's hand, "So now we have a different worst case scenario."

"It'll be all right." Walstib pulled out his com-phone, "Contact Lab. Please."

An hour later, the HyperRider had landed in the field behind the assembly facility and the entire group was busy attaching one of the nuclear rockets to the back. The sounds of plasma cutters, wrenches, drills and other assorted tools went on for hours. Finally, new connections, wiring, cowling, and other parts had been attached.

Fissile said, "One more turn of the torque wrench…there. That should do it."

The HyperRider's new nuclear engine was now fully attached.

Anne looked at Walstib, "Maybe I should have thought of this earlier. But we've only seen the HyperRider launch using the magnetic launcher. How are you going to launch it this time?"

"It can launch, like the Shuttle Bus, from hover mode. Not nearly as fast, but we're not looking for a fast launch here," replied Walstib.

As Walstib climbed into the door of the HyperRider, he turned to look back at the group. Everyone looked a little pensive.

Walstib said, "Not to worry. You've all done a great job. Now it's time to give it a spin around the block. Go have dinner. I'll be back before you know it."

Fissile smiled and said, "If you go fast enough, you'll be back before we know you've left."

Everyone cocked their heads with a quizzical look on their faces, then looked to Walstib for an answer.

Walstib held up his hands in front of him, "Don't look at me. I still can't figure out that space-time continuum thing."

Walstib turned back into the HyperRider and closed the door.

Everyone pulled some scaffolding or a tool away from the scramjet, backed away, and waved.

Walstib waved from the pilot's seat, pushed a few buttons, and the HyperRider moved into a hover. It was slightly heavier than before with the addition of the new nuclear engine. Slowly it took off.

The HyperRider gained speed and remained in scramjet mode until it broke free of Earth's atmosphere. Walstib looked at the air speed indicator, it showed 'Mach 17'. "Time to kick it up a notch," he thought. He pushed the button marked 'Nuclear Engine'. The nuclear engine kicked in. The HyperRider, now no longer in scramjet mode, blasted forward. Walstib looked at the instrument panel, the air speed indicator showed 'Mach 20', then '30', then '40'. Walstib allowed himself a little laugh. "We're going to need a bigger speedometer."

The early NASA Apollo missions got to Mach 4 on their way to the moon.

The HyperRider shot by the Moon.

NASA's New Horizon satellite mission to Pluto in 2015 reached Mach 48. The Orion program, with nuclear pulse drive, as envisioned in 1955, was projected to get to Mach 90.

The HyperRider, being propelled by Fissile's new nuclear design was now hurtling along at Mach 400. A few minutes later it whizzed by Mars. Walstib looked out the window at the beautiful scene, but Mars was gone in just a few seconds. Walstib spoke to the cockpit voice recorder, "Engine holding up. Stable control process. Try steering."

He aimed for Jupiter. The HyperRider was now at Mach 600. A few minutes later he shot past Jupiter. "Steering good." Then he laughed and said, "Closed course. Professional driver. Do not attempt at home." He steered toward Saturn. "Driver feeling fine."

Walstib was distracted by a glint to his left and looked over. He saw a small UFO flying alongside the HyperRider.

The little green alien pilot looked over at Walstib and gave the "Do you want to race?" gesture by pointing his finger forward.

Walstib looked forward, shook his head to clear his mind, then looked to the left again. The alien grinned. Walstib shook his head "No."

The UFO pilot scowled and waved off Walstib in disgust with the back of his hand. The UFO streaked away.

Walstib blinked and rubbed his eyes. He looked back over to the left. Nothing there.

Walstib said aloud, "OhhKayyy, maybe it's time to turn around."

The HyperRider re-entered the Earth's atmosphere and, back in scramjet mode, headed straight for Russia. It hovered to a landing back in the field. Fissile, Mae, and the Sci Crew had been too nervous to eat dinner. They had been inside going over all the details of the project. Everyone heard the landing and ran outside. They applauded as the HyperRider's door opened. Walstib climbed out.

Mae was first to blurt out a question, "Dad, are you OK?"

"I'm fine. I'm fine. Starving, but fine."

Fissile said, "We couldn't eat. We're starving too. Let's go grab dinner and hear about your trip and the engine test run."

As they walked over to the Shuttle Bus, Walstib looked at the group, "You know it's true."

Everyone looked quizzical.

Mae asked, "What is Dad?"

"They're out there."

Fissile smiled, "Over dinner I'll explain weightlessness and blood flow to the brain."

CHAPTER 58

During their dinner at the diner, the group listened intently to every detail of the test flight.

"So, to summarize, you'd give the design a thumbs up?" asked Fissile.

"Absolutely. Smooth take-off and no vibrations at full throttle," responded Walstib.

"No need for any modifications?"

"None."

Fissile looked at Anne and Neil, "Are we sure we have enough rocket bodies and nuclear engines for the task?"

Anne and Neil nodded yes.

Fissile stated, "Good. Then let's proceed with final assembly."

Walstib looked at Mae, Ellie, and Yang, "Are you confident in the design of the nano-tubing spooling device?"

They also nodded yes.

"Good. Let's proceed with the spooling process. I'll call the lab and have the Sticky Bots refitted with steering rockets. We'll send the HyperRider to pick them up tomorrow."

The three terrorists had been watching the facility through binoculars from the main road. Their leader said, "OK. The number of cars that have left is the same as the number that went in this morning. The lights are out. It must be clear of employees. Let's go in." They got in their car and drove to the facility. They walked to the front door and used a high-tech electronic device to unlock the door.

An alarm went off on Walstib's com-phone and he pulled it out of his pocket. He pushed a button and he could see the interior of the facility.

"What's wrong?" asked Mae.

"Don't know. But let's watch," said Walstib, as he pulled out two thin wires to create a screen so everyone could see.

The terrorists walked briskly through the facility and scanned quickly left and right for their prized nukers.

"Hey what's this?" screamed one of the terrorists.

"What the …." yelled the second one.

Before he could turn to look back, the head terrorist had been hit too. They were being hit from all directions by streams of spider webbing emanating from the biggest spiders they had ever seen. They were covered from head to toe, and their attempts to run just made them fall over.

"That's amazing," beamed Walstib. "How did that happen?"

Ellie looked at Mae and Yang, "We realized that Peter couldn't guard the facility by himself 24-7, so we called your friend Dr. Pod. He told us how to train the spiders."

"Which we did while we were working on the web spooling device," added Yang.

Anne grinned, "If we didn't need to be so secretive, we could send this in to 'World's Dumbest Crooks, Episode 549'. "

CHAPTER 69

The next morning, at the facility, the group stood by the front door.

The local police were hauling away the three terrorists.

"We're going to have to be more vigilant," said Fissile.

"Sad, but true," murmured Walstib. "I thought that type of anger and hatred was a thing of the past."

The previous week had been busy - the rocket engines were finalized, the web spooling was finalized, the Space Bots had been delivered, and all three items had been installed in the rockets. In addition, the trucks that had initially delivered all the parts and material had been retrofitted to haul the final rocket assembly to the launch site. Walstib had arranged with President Tereshkova to lease a nearby launch site.

Finally, the trucks were loaded and the convoy to the launch pad pulled out of the assembly facility. Peter Black led the way in the City Trekker, followed by the twelve trucks, followed by six Elektrostal police cars, with Donna and Keith's catering truck taking up the rear. Walstib, Fissile, Mae, and the Sci Crew followed overhead in the Shuttle Bus.

As they flew, Anne looked out the window, "This is beautiful countryside. Wally, you really are a good tour guide."

"And you all make a good tour group," Walstib responded. "How about a nice game of 'I Spy with My Little Eye'?"

"Dad, no," protested Mae.

"How come you use lots of the same size small engines in the Shuttle Bus and the HyperRider? And why not one medium size for the Shuttle Bus and one big one for the HyperRider?" inquired Neil.

"Give it a rest," Anne poked Neil in the ribs. "Enjoy the view."

"I'm curious."

Walstib turned his head toward Neil for a second, "There are three reasons. First, economies of scale in design and manufacturing. Second, safety in redundancy. And third, each one can turn slightly to aid in steering. Don't they teach you the practical applications of engineering in school?"

"So far it's mostly textbook stuff," Yang commented.

"Practical applications are half the battle. That was the key point in Rodney Dangerfield's classic film 'Back to School'."

"Besides the humor," added Mae.

"Wally, how come you always say 'Please' when you talk to your com-system or com-phone?" asked Ellie.

There was a pause. "When I was first starting my own business and programming all the systems, I used my wife's, Mae's mother's, voice for the computer. She passed away a few years ago, but now when I talk to any of the systems, I feel like I am still talking with her."

Mae put her hand on her dad's shoulder.

The cabin was quiet for a few minutes.

Yang started it off, "Teflon."

"Steam engine," said Anne.

"Steam engine?" quizzed Yang.

"You caught me off guard," protested Anne.

Mae looked to see if it was her turn, "Sewing machine."

Ellie jumped in with, "Plastic."

"Photographic film," said Neil.

"The plow," added Fissile.

Everyone waited for Walstib.

"Air conditioning."

"AC's a good one," said Anne.

"When you live in the jungle, it's a great one," smiled Mae.

"We have a winner for this round. One point for Wally," said Yang.

The rest of the trip was quiet as everyone relaxed and looked out of the windows.

CHAPTER 60

The convoy arrived at the launch site in Plesetsk, north of Moscow. They pulled up to the gates and the Shuttle Bus landed near the front of the convoy. Walstib walked over to the gates as they were swung open by a tall man with short white hair. "Hello, I'm Dr. Walstib."

"Hello, Dr. Walstib, President Tereshkova said you might need some help. I'm John Bander, the Launch Director, and," he waved his hand behind him, "this is my launch team."

Behind the Launch Director were about fifty people in uniforms, all looked enthusiastic.

"We are very glad you're here," said Walstib.

"We were afraid this facility would never see another launch. How many other launch sites have you used?"

"Zero. How many launches have you directed here?"

"Seventy three."

"Let me revise my earlier statement. We are very, very glad to have your help."

"We're happy to help. Please come in."

Walstib waved for the trucks to continue into the launch area. After the last truck entered, the police Chief pulled up and whispered to Walstib, "We'll stick around until you complete the launch."

"Thanks, that's a big sense of comfort."

The catering truck pulled up and Donna rolled down the window, "We'll just pull in, in case anyone gets hungry."

Walstib smiled, "Once they smell the food they'll get hungry."

Fissile, Mae, and the Sci Crew joined up with Walstib.

"Let me show you the control room while my team sets up your rockets," motioned Bander.

As they walked into the launch area they saw the fifteen launch pads with launch towers and about fifty launch personnel. The launch teams gave signals to the truck drivers to pull up to their respective launch pads.

They entered the control room and the group saw one wall had a large, blast-proof, viewing window, and in the center of the room were rows of consoles with hundreds of switches, monitors, and headsets. The far wall had a collection of pictures, including Marvin the Martian, R2-D2, Gort, and Robot from 'Lost in Space'.

Walstib looked at Bander, "Someone has a sense of humor."

Bander replied, "That is our Wall of Fame. Someday, if we do our jobs right today, our grandchildren may meet others out there."

"I have no doubt," smiled Walstib. He turned to Mae and the Sci Crew, "Please, go help the launch team set up the rockets, I'll finalize the launch and guidance software and download it to their consoles."

At the end of the day, the Launch Director reported to Walstib with Sci Crew in tow. "Launch pad is ready, and I've called the local airports to clear the airspace."

Walstib said, "Good, the software is ready."

Bander spoke into the microphone, "Clear the launch pad."

After a few minutes the Launch Pad Team arrived in the Control Room and sat at their consoles.

The Launch Pad Team, now the Control Room Team, put on their headsets, flicked toggle switches, and reviewed their monitors.

The Launch Leader called out, "Rocket Number One and Launch Pad Number One. Ready?"

The Control Room Team member responsible for Rocket and Pad Number One gave a visual thumbs up and a verbal "Go."

Bander repeated the process for each rocket and each launch pad. After he received twelve approvals, he looked at Walstib and pointed to the main console, "You are *go for launch*. There's the launch button. Push it when you're ready."

"Gather 'round, Phase Two Launch Team," glowed Walstib.

Everyone went over to the red launch button.

Walstib's hand was poised over the button, "Count down please."

Mae started, "Five."

Ellie, "Four."

Anne, "Three."

Yang, "Two."

Neil, "One."

Fissile, "Launch!"

Walstib pushed the button.

All twelve rockets lifted off.

Both the Plesetsk and the Phase Two Launch Teams cheered and whistled.

Bander commented to Walstib, "I don't miss the smelly smoke trails of our usual chemical rockets."

The doors to the Control Room burst open. Everyone turned and looked.

Donna announced, "Did someone order a Happy Launch Day cake?"

Keith pushed in a huge catering trolley with a massive cake. The top of the cake was aglow with twelve candles.

CHAPTER 61

After the cake, everyone in the control room was full and exhausted. The Launch Control Team, one by one, started to fall asleep in their chairs or placed their heads on their consoles. They had done this before.

Walstib, Fissile, Mae and the Sci Crew were wide awake. They watched the monitors.

As the rockets broke through the Earth's atmosphere, the cameras and location beacons embedded in each rocket came on. The rockets roared out of Earth's gravitational pull and veered off into space. As they headed out, they stayed in their circular pattern.

Everyone on the Phase Two Team watched the main screen that now showed twelve sub-screens. There was an additional screen off to the side that had a map of Earth's solar system. The map background was black, with gray dots indicating the trajectory of the outbound rockets, and gold dots indicating the trajectory of the inbound comet.

In about the same time it took Walstib's test flight to get to Jupiter, the rockets arrived at their destination. All 12 rockets veered out slightly to form a larger circular formation. The rockets then ceased firing. Side jets fired gently and brought the rockets to a stop. The side jets swiveled, fired briefly, and turned the rockets around 180 degrees, remaining in a circular formation. Capsule doors on each rocket slid open, and from each, out popped several newly configured Space Bots. The bots darted diagonally across the center of the circle toward the opposing rocket. Each bot trailed a strand of the spider silk and nano-tubing webbing. Once they reached the far rocket, the bots used their mechanical arms to secure the webbing to the hooks that had sprung up from the open door. Each bot went back and forth several times and formed a huge five kilometer-wide net. The multiple strands added redundancy in case one or more strands broke during the capture process. The web was complete and in place. The bots clambered back into the capsule doors. Eleven doors closed. There was a pause. The twelfth bot, perched inside the capsule, extended its mechanical arm and gave the door a quick rap with its mechanical hand. The door slid shut.

On the screen in the control room, the rocket and web formation dotted lines were now blinking stationary dots. The comet's dotted line was getting closer to the accurately situated web. On the camera screens, the team watched as the comet came into view.
Walstib woke up the Launch Director and said, "Your team may want to watch this."
John Bander took one look at the screens and realized his team would. He went to each consol and woke them up.
The comet came closer, closer, closer, until finally the comet was snared by the webbing. It was a direct hit. The laser sensors had targeted the comet and signaled the rocket thrusters to give micro-bursts in order to maneuver the web into place. The comet continued on its trajectory with the rockets now trailing behind.
The screen showed the path of the comet on its original trajectory, to swing by the moon.

Six rockets on one side fired momentarily altering the comet's course ever so slightly. This far out, only a slight course correction was needed.

The gold dots on the screen moved, reflecting the course correction. The comet was now on a straight line to the Moon.

In the control room, all eyes were on the screen. A few on the launch Team crossed their fingers.

The comet, webbing, and rockets hurtled through space. As the comet passed Mars, all twelve rockets briefly fired simultaneously, slowing the comet slightly.

On the screen, the gold dot was now close to the Moon.

The rockets fired briefly again. The doors on the capsules slid open, and the bots came out. They snipped the webbing where it was attached to the rockets, cutting the comet loose.

The comet sailed on but much slower than before.

The rockets fired again and brought them to a standstill, where they would be retrieved later.

The comet continued along.

On the screen the gold dot was almost touching the Moon. The comet continued on its path now more in the Moon's gravitational pull than on its own momentum.

The comet and the Moon were now very, very close.

And then impact. It was a massive explosion. Moon dust and comet dust erupted upward and in all directions. The dust obscured the view of the Moon.

Neil looked at Anne, Ellie, Mae, and Yang and mouthed, "Wildly amazing."

CHAPTER 62

Bander came over to the Phase Two Team, "Congratulations! You have done what mankind has dreamed of for centuries, given life to the Moon!"

Walstib gave a huge smile, "Thanks. But the credit for the idea belongs to Neil, Yang, Ellie, Anne, and Mae. And thank you. We couldn't have done this without you and your team."

"Keep us in mind for your next event. We do fireworks, too."

The Phase Two Team all laughed.

Bander continued, "Your drivers and security team are welcome to stay in our quarters for the night. They probably shouldn't drive back with the little sleep we all got."

"That sounds great. I'm sure they'd appreciate it. We're," Walstib gestured to the Phase Two team, "going to fly back, it will only take us a few minutes."

"I'll go let them know."

"Thanks," said Walstib as he gave Bander a heartfelt handshake.

Fissile looked at Walstib, Mae, and the Sci Crew, "What now?"

"We have to allow time for the Moon to settle out, but in the meantime we really have some work to do."

"Such as?"

"We have to build the initial solar panels for the start-up energy system. We'll build more panels out of Moon materials once we have built the initial infrastructure."

Neil added, "We also have to construct the initial regolith diggers to get at the minerals in the Moon soil. We'll dig for silicon for the solar panels and titanium for building materials."

"And we'll need to bring up hydroponic gardens for food," said Ellie.

"And build several more HyperRiders," Anne added, while pulling back on an imaginary joystick.

Yang sounded introspective, "And launch tonnes of nitrogen to seed the Moon's atmosphere, currently overly oxygen rich, so it will be compatible with our needs."

"I can help secure more nuclear material and build more launch vehicles. That is if you'd like my help," said Fissile

"We're counting on it," said Walstib. "I'm exhausted. Shall we head back to Hotel Fissile?"

They left the Control Room and walked to the Shuttle Bus in tired silence.

Once they were airborne, Neil asked the question on everyone's mind, "We'd love to help, but we're supposed to start college soon. We want to go to college, but expanding mankind's reach into space somehow seems more important than Poetry 101. What should we do?"

Walstib paused for a moment before responding, "You'll learn more on this project in the next year about math, engineering, chemistry, physics, biology and geology than in twenty years in college. In fact, I'll make sure your universities give you credit for the work here. However, college is about more than just the classes in your field of pursuit. To be well rounded, there are decas of other courses you will need that I can't teach you, like poetry, art,

history, etc. Plus college is half about learning social skills, making contacts, and learning who you are as a person." Anne reached out and touched each of her Sci Crew mates and said, "Why don't we work with you until Phase Two is complete and then we'll go to college?"
Walstib smiled, "I was hoping you'd say that."

CHAPTER 63

One Day Later
Billions of tonnes of ice had struck the moon. The ice was instantly vaporized, some of it turned into an oxygen rich atmosphere and some coalesced into water and formed micro lakes in the thousands of craters. The gold core was scattered over thousands of kilometers.

Two Months Later
Thousands of nitrogen canisters had been launched and flown over the Moon. The nitrogen was sprayed out and mixed with the oxygen. The mixture reasonably approximated the Earth's atmosphere. Enough so to make the Moon habitable. The new atmosphere and the thousands of micro lakes helped to somewhat even out the Moon's temperature fluctuations.

Six Months Later
Walstib, Fissile, Mae, and the Sci Crew had spent the last few months designing and making the initial infrastructure for the first phase of manufacturing, food production, and living quarters.

During this time, several more HyperRiders, with the additional nuclear propulsion, were constructed. The design of the original HyperRider was duplicated and Walstib's automated manufacturing shop allowed for an amazingly fast build time.

Eight Months Later

The last few months had been spent shuttling material and initial infrastructure to the Moon via their new HyperRiders. Everyone had their own now. Racing HyperRiders to the Moon, in retrospect, was probably a bad idea. It was only the second time anyone had heard Walstib raise his voice. The coolest thing they had ever done, but fairly dangerous.

Twelve Months Later

Moon City was complete. It wasn't really a city and it wasn't really complete. However, it was simple to build and functional. Massive composite tubes, manufactured on the Moon, had been half buried horizontally in trenches and covered with regolith. This protected the inhabitants from solar flares, micro asteroids that slipped past the laser cannon protection system, and temperature fluctuations. The tubes were laid out spoke and wheel fashion. In the center of the hubs were vertical tubes that allowed for viewing. It was a start.

Walstib, Mae, and the Sci Crew had spent most of the last year in the Brazil Lab, but flew frequently to Russia for launches. One of the side benefits to being in Russia was that Fissile had outfitted the formal dining hall in his house as a music recording studio. Whenever Neil, Yang, Ellie, Anne, and Mae had any downtime, they jammed, much to Fissile's delight.

CHAPTER 64

As his HyperRider hovered over the Moon, Walstib could see the results of all the hard work over the past year. He hovered down to the landing pad, paved to prevent the fine lunar soil from kicking up under the powerful engines. The door opened and Walstib stepped out, followed by Presidents Dire, Filho, and Tereshkova. "Right this way, please," motioned Walstib. He escorted the three presidents over to a small, elevated viewing area.

Mae, Neil, Ellie, and Anne were already there.

"Where's Yang?" whispered Walstib.

Ellie whispered back, "He'll be here in a minute." She looked over at the landing pad, "Oh, here he is now."

Yang's HyperRider landed. Yang stepped out, followed by the female news reporter they had met at the science quiz bowl a year ago. They walked over to the others, Yang joined the Sci Crew, and the reporter stood over to the side. Walstib cleared his throat, then spoke, "Greetings President Dire, President Filho, and President Tereshkova. Welcome to the Moon, or as we like to call it 'Phase Two'. As you can see it is slightly different than a year ago." He pointed over to a few small buildings. "We have several square kilometers of solar panels powering research labs, manufacturing facilities, mining operations, hydroponic gardens, recreation areas, living quarters, and a hotel. The people you see before you, Neil, Yang, Anne, Ellie, and Mae, are to be congratulated for coming up with this amazing idea." A Cam Bot swooped in and took a picture. Walstib gave a broad genuine smile, then turned back to the presidents. "And we couldn't have done this without your help. You three are our first guests and we ask that you cut the official opening ribbon to Phase Two of humankind's home in the solar system. Please take these scissors, made of titanium mined from the Moon's surface, and cut the ribbon."

He handed them each a scissors, and they posed just long enough for the Cam Bot to snap a photo before they cut the ribbon. The ribbon fluttered down a little slower than back on Earth.

Walstib and the others applauded.

The Sci Crew came over to Walstib, and Yang signaled for the reporter to join them.

Yang made the introductions, "Dr. Walstib, this is Mary Lanta," and he turned to the reporter, "Mary this is Dr. Walstib." He turned back to Walstib, "She's a reporter."

"Nice to meet you Mary. Perhaps Yang forgot to mention this to you, but I don't do interviews."

"And I flew all this way just to ask you who you're wearing," Mary shot back.

Mae and the Sci Crew stepped forward.

"Dad, you've accomplished so much, people want to know about you," said Mae as she held his arm.

"You've inspired us. It might be good for the world if you'd inspire more people," said Anne.

"Go ahead," interjected the President of Brazil with a grin, "we give interviews all the time, and most people don't listen to us. I think everyone would listen to you."

Walstib looked at Mae and the Sci Crew, "OK… But you have to take these three politicians off my hands and take them for a tour." And he added in a stage whisper, "They don't stop talking."

Neil spoke up, "Follow us please."

Walstib gestured to the benches at the viewing area and he and Mary each took a seat.

Before Mary started, she reached into her bag and pulled out a box. She opened the box, turned on a Fly Cam with dual cameras, and released it. It hovered between them and filmed both.

As Walstib and Mary started their interview, the Sci Crew and Mae helped the three presidents board the Moon Trekker. The Moon Trekker was a standard Jungle Trekker but with the roof and windows removed. Yang drove off slowly.

Mary hoisted her microphone. "Good evening. I'm Mary Lanta. Tonight we are pleased to bring you the first interview ever with Dr. Walstib. Thank you Dr. Walstib for allowing us to talk with you in this lovely setting."

"Well, as you know, I'm delighted to be here."

Mary thought it best if she started off with small talk, "I hope this is the first of many Moon cities to come."

"I don't think we have any plans, but we can certainly expand if needed."

"Expansion of the human habitat seems to be the theme of this endeavor. What was the inspiration for this undertaking?"

"This undertaking was the brainchild of my colleagues Mae, Neil, Anne, Ellie, and Yang. I suppose the model they based this project on was the theory of the origins of water and life on our planet. We speculate that several billion years ago a massive icy comet from the frozen outer reaches of our solar system collided with Earth. Its ice turned into water and oxygen. The water became a massive ocean, called Panthalassa, which covered the globe. The comet's core created a large single land mass, or Super Continent, known as Pangaea, which is ancient Greek for One World. It has since split up, due to the rotation of the Earth, into the continents as we know them today. That event just seemed like 'Phase One' to us, and thus our plan to do the same to the Moon simply became 'Phase Two'."

Neil started the tour, "We have ten main areas here at our first Moon City. The solar electric area, the mining area, and manufacturing area are just outside the city. Inside the city is a tourist hotel, a housing area, a laboratory, a garden, and a recreation area."

First, they drove past the solar farm and saw the kilometers of panels. When observing the solar panels, the Russian President cracked a joke, "I like solar so much I had two sons." They all laughed even though they had heard that joke many times before.

Second, they drove past the mining area with hundreds of small autonomous scooper trucks, like front-end loaders, scooping up the top inch of regolith and hoisting the load into the carrier section. The Scoopers went back to the sorting area where silicon, titanium, and other minerals, including the gold, were separated. The Brazilian President asked, "What happens to the gold?"

Neil answered, "Half the gold we mine pays for the operations of the Moon Base. And the other half goes to hiring a million teachers to fan out around the world to

teach reading and writing. For the first time in the world's history, literacy will reach one hundred percent."
The three presidents all nodded approvingly.

"Dr. Walstib, on a personal note, you were the youngest ever to graduate from MIT. You have four Ph.D.s, you have 1802 patents, you invented the first ultra low cost solar panel, which is now used to provide electricity to more than half the homes on the planet, sales of which made you the wealthiest man in the world. And you have designed a video game that sold over one hundred million copies. I know the kids out there will know this. What was the name of it?"
"Thomas the Tank Engine and His Little Turtle Buddies Help Rebuild Terrapin Station."
"That's a mouthful."
"I was six when I designed it."

They drove to the third area, the manufacturing area where bots built the tubes, the solar panels, and most of the additional infrastructure needed to make Moon City operational.
Mae, Yang, Ellie, Anne, and Neil had each taken turns giving descriptions of the various areas.
After the main part of the tour was completed, Anne put on her best tour guide voice, "We saved the best for last. Are you ready for the Recreation Area?"
All three presidents said a resounding "Yes."
They drove over to the Recreation Area and everyone climbed out of the Moon Trekker.

The first sport was a standard size basketball court, but the hoops were set at six meters instead of the standard three meters. Yang picked up a basketball from a storage rack on the side of the court, took a few quick strides, leapt way up in the air and dunked the ball. "Anyone up for Low Gravity B-Ball?"
All three presidents demurred.

"You've never given an interview before. Why are you breaking your silence now?"
"Well Mary, we've reached an important turning point. Fewer students than ever are signing up for math, science, and engineering. If I hadn't studied these subjects, I could never have invented so much cool stuff. We need more kids to get into science. We need more scientists to find more cures for people. We need more scientists to invent better satellites to give us earlier warnings for hurricanes. We still haven't figured out how to detect earthquakes. I think a lot of people think we have things pretty well in hand, so why bother. But, there are thousands of things that new scientists and engineers could improve upon, or even invent things no one has thought of.
We really need to focus more on inventing and discovery. Did you know that out of the thousands of public schools in the U.S. there are only six named after Albert Einstein?"
Mary looked shocked, "That's just sad."
"There is so much more that we could be doing. We need better science labs in schools, the list goes on. Primarily, we want every student to start thinking beyond the horizon. Like the early explorers. They were told nothing was beyond the horizon. They dreamed there was something.

They went after it, and there was something beyond the horizon."

"I think we can all get behind your suggestions. Here's another question. People might not see the difference between your Phase Two project and Leake's approach. What was the difference?"

"Our approach was to have the results of the project benefit all mankind. We brought water to an otherwise uninhabitable body. The comet was originally on a path between the Moon and the Earth. We actually steered its path to veer farther away from the Earth to collide with the moon. In the unlikely event that anything would have gone wrong, it would have done so at a safe distance. Leake was going to bring the comet so close to the Earth, in order to keep mining retrieval costs to a minimum, that it could have been drawn into our gravitational field and collided with the Earth. All for his own enrichment. And his alone."

"Well thanks to you, your daughter and the Sci Crew, we are safe and better off. OK, here is one final burning question. You are somewhat of a mystery. We know nothing of your background. What kind of name is Walstib?"

Walstib hesitated a moment, then responded with, "Gosh Mary...it's...it's a last name."

"But we have heard there are no birth records, and that you named yourself after your company 'Worldwide Analytic and Logistic Systems'…"

Walstib cut in, "No, no. I assure you I didn't name myself after my company."

"Well folks, there you have it. A tiny glimpse into the man of the hour. The man who dreamed beyond the horizon and

brought us Phase Two. Thanks for watching, this has been Mary Lanta reporting from the Moon."
Mary turned off her mic and shut down the Fly Cam. She looked at Walstib and smiled, "That wasn't so bad was it?"
"You made it seem easy, but I couldn't tell you everything now or I wouldn't get a second interview." He smiled.
"OK, you're on, just let me know when."
"Well, not now, because now you have to help me cook dinner for the official guests."

They moved on to the next sport. Ellie hopped into a convertible version of the egg shaped Capture Trekker, now renamed Crater Trekker. She revved it, shot forward toward the nearest crater, used the front slope as a ramp, and soared clear over the crater. She landed safely on the other side and shouted, "Woohoooo." She came skittering back to the group and, still pumped, said "Who's next?"
All three presidents demurred again.
They walked a few more meters to the golf driving range.
"Ah, this is more my style," smiled President Tereshkova. She picked up a driver and a ball from the storage rack, placed the ball in the rubber tee, and took a couple of practice swings. She addressed the ball then took a full swing. The ball went straight as an arrow and hit the five hundred meter marker. "Wow," she said "let me know when you have a full course built."

President Filho picked out a ball and stepped up to the tee. He borrowed the driver from Tereshkova, took a quick practice swing, then let one fly. The ball sailed past the six hundred meter marker but they couldn't see it land. "Hey, where'd my ball go?"

"They don't bounce up here. It burrowed into the regolith. We're going to have to work on that, maybe embed a homing beacon in each ball," apologized Neil.

"That's all right, I'll still have a go at it," said President Dire. He took a new ball, the last one, and the club and got up to the tee. "I believe in trying to speed up the game. No practice swing for me." He took a huge swing. The ball went forward about ten meters and about one hundred meters to the right. "Blast it, hooked it again. That was the last ball. Sorry, sorry. I'll go get it." He took off toward the walled off area where the ball landed.

"Wait, Sir," shouted Anne. "That's a restricted area."

"I'm sure I have authorization," shouted Dire over his shoulder.

"That's not the point," Anne said under her breath as she started to run after him.

Dire reached the walled off area, opened the large door, and ran in. A moment later he looked down at green slime crawling up his leg, and then everyone heard a very anguished, "Aaahhgg."

Anne reached the wall and climbed the stairs to the external catwalk used for viewing into the compound. She looked down at a very nervous President. "Don't move, Sir. I'll be right in."

She climbed down the stairs, went to a storage locker by the door, put on a pair of thigh high boots, and grabbed a second larger pair. She entered the door and saw Dire surrounded by a range of extraordinary primeval looking plants and creatures: moving vines, huge colorful flowers, undulating green slime, three meter long slugs, and two meter long walking jellyfish. Not only was he standing in the ooze but a three meter tall Venus fly trap type plant was slowly leaning in his direction.

She walked over to Dire and placed his boots next to him. The slime moved away from the coating on the boots. "Lift your right foot up," she held his arm for support, "and slowly move it to the boot. As your foot gets near the boot the slime will come off." As predicted the slime retreated. "Good. Now put your foot into the boot and do the same with your left foot."

They slowly walked back outside, closed the door, and took off their boots.

By then the others had gathered around.

"What is this place?" asked Dire.

"This is our Ecological Research Area. Some of the stuff in there is friendly, some isn't."

Dire looked down at his leg, touched his shin, then pulled up a pant leg. "Hey I had a cut there and now it's almost healed. What did that slime do to my leg?"

"Leaches back on Earth help heal cuts, but this stuff actually seeks out cuts. Can you imagine how this will help advance medicine? Some of the stuff we've found up here is amazing," said Anne.

"How did all this stuff get here?" asked Filho.

Neil answered, "We speculate that there's life all over the galaxy, much of it dormant. It just needs to find the right environment in which to grow. The original ingredients were on the comet. Once they got to the right temperature and oxygen levels here on the Moon, they started to grow."

President Tereshkova asked, "It's been on that comet for years?"

Ellie commented, "Archeologists have found grains of wheat in clay urns in Egyptian tombs that were over five thousand years old, and when they put the grain in soil, it grew. *And*, scientists have found bacteria in ice core samples in the Arctic that were thirty two thousand years old. When they thawed the ice, the bacteria started to wiggle."

Dire commented, "But there wasn't any soil up here when the comet landed."

Mae jumped in, "We've been bringing up our own soil. We composted yard waste, food waste, and sewage waste together. You know, people just throw that stuff away. Then we ran it through a solar trough to neutralize any contaminants from Earth and made it completely inert. We had it piled here originally to grow trees, which we are still in the process of doing."

Filho asked, "Wouldn't the impact destroy any life forms?"

"NASA tested that by spinning nematode worms in a centrifuge up to 2000 Gs, to simulate impact forces, and they survived.

Anne concluded, "If everyone's OK, let's go have dinner, where I promise, nothing will bite back."

They climbed back on the Moon Trekker and made their way back to the dining hall.

Walstib and Mary had cooked up a fabulous dinner. Walstib greeted them, "Welcome to the dining hall. Please have a seat. We hope you enjoy the meal. As you might imagine, we are big proponents of locally-grown."

Mary asked the group, "I haven't been there yet, how was the recreational area?"

Filho laughed, "The Guinness people are going to have to write a whole new book."

Everyone enjoyed the meal and the lively discussions. Walstib told Mary she could help him host dinners anytime. She was as adept in her political knowledge as she was in her science.

After the meal, Walstib stood up, thanked his four guests for coming, and said that he would escort Mary and the three presidents next door to the hotel. He explained it was getting late and that he, Mae, and the Sci Crew had a meeting to go to. He wished everyone a good night's sleep before tomorrow's departure.

CHAPTER 65

After they had said good night to their guests, Walstib, Mae, and the Sci Crew walked over to the landing pad and climbed aboard Walstib's HyperRider. No one said a word. They were all too excited.

Walstib hovered up and then shot forward. He pushed a few buttons and "Mountains of the Moon" came up on the sound system. Everyone appreciated the choice.

The HyperRider skimmed across the Moon's surface, extraordinarily beautiful even in its starkness. After a few minutes they passed from the light side to dark side.

Anne broke the silence, in her deepest voice she said, "Neil…come over to the dark side."

Yang asked, "Didn't she say that same joke last night as we crossed?"

Neil said softly, "Sadly, yes."

The HyperRider lights were on guiding their way as they continued to skim across the Moon's surface.

Mae turned to her dad and whispered, "So?"

Walstib, looked at Mae, "What?"

"How did the interview go?"

Walstib smiled, "She's pretty nice. If that's what you're asking."

Mae patted her dad's arm, "Yup."

In the distance they could see a few lights. After a few minutes they arrived and landed. They climbed out and went into the facility where they were greeted by Fissile, Dr. Pod, and Bander. A few launch operators, already seated with headphones on, waved.

The Moon Launch Facility was designed to mimic the high tech facility in Russia, with a viewing window on one side, consoles and monitors in the middle, and on the back wall a few new pictures, including Jimmy Neutron and a group shot of Tribbles.

They looked out at the launch pad where a hundred rockets were gleaming under the lights.

Walstib asked, "Are we ready?"

Bander smiled at Walstib, "Yes, Sir. We've already been through the checklist. Everything is go for launch."

Walstib walked over to the big red launch button, "Everyone gather 'round. We're going to do it a little differently this time. Mae, Neil, Ellie, Anne, Yang, Dr. Fissile put your hands on the launch button. This time I get to do the countdown."

They all nodded.

"Countdown, please," said Bander.

Walstib, in a very happy tone, "Five. Four. Three. Two. One. Launch."

All hands pushed the button.

What a glorious sight. All one hundred rockets shot upward.

The launch team cheered and whistled.

Walstib, almost tearing up, said, "Thank you, Phase Three Team. Mars…here we come."

Keith and Donna came out of the back room wheeling in a cart. "We have a special launch celebration dessert for you!" beamed Donna. "You won't believe how fluffy we can get our Moon Meringues in low gravity."

CHAPTER 66

Two Months Later

It was just dusk, and some lights were on in the old hangar at an old abandoned airfield. There were many old airfields these days as the new AeroLifter airfields needed much more landing room.

Inside, Neil, Anne, Ellie, Mae, and Yang were sitting in some old chairs and sofas in the back. A few meters next to them were some tables and chairs with computers and monitors which were next to several storage racks spilling over with tools and equipment. In the front of the hangar was the Sci Crew airship, inflated and tethered.

Yang stood up, "Come on, we should get going."

Ellie said calmly, "We have plenty of time."

"I just don't want to be late for our first gig."

Mae's com-phone rang, she answered, "Hi Daddy."

Walstib was in his lab and sounded happy, "I got your present, I love it. I'm wearing it, take a look."

Mae put her com-phone on the table and pulled out the two little wires to create a large screen. "Guys, take a look."

They could see his new shirt which they had made up. It read 'Wally's Five Star Tours'.

They all smiled.

"Thank you. It's perfect."

Neil leaned in, "It's the least we could do. Thank you for the hangar."

"And thanks for arranging for us all to be at the same university," said Ellie.

"It would have been very strange being away from the team," said Anne. "This is delightful."

"Speaking of college, how was your first week?"

Mae gushed, "It was great. We had History, English, Philosophy, Marketing, and that Poetry thing."

"I got something else in the mail today, a letter."

"Who sends letters anymore?" asked Mae.

"I don't know. The return address just says it's from a prison. Hold on, let me open it."

Walstib opened the letter and laughed.

"What?"

"It's from our buddy, Charlie Leake. He says, 'You have stolen my idea. At a minimum I want all the gold, plus naming rights. The moon rightfully should be named after me. If you don't respond by….' Blah, blah, blah, the rest is all legal mumbo jumbo."

"Throw that in the compost and we'll take the soil to the Moon. That way his name will be on the Moon," suggested Yang.

"Good idea."

Mae spoke up, "We've got to run, we're playing at a club tonight."

"Where?"

"Woody Mingle's Blues Club. Fissile set it up."

"I'll hook in and watch from here. Bye bye."

Everyone said goodbye.

They hung up.

They put on their riding jackets and walked out of the small front door. Out in the parking lot there were now five Tryx, all with new license plates that read, SciCrew1, SciCrew2,

SciCrew3, SciCrew4, and SciCrew5. They each hopped on and headed downtown for the club. They had rehearsed there for weeks, knew all the back roads to the club, and made good time.

They arrived at the club, went in the musicians' entrance, and were greeted by Fissile. "Instruments are all tuned up and ready," said Fissile. "A comedian is warming up the crowd. He's pretty funny if you want to listen."
Instead, they told him about the letter from Leake.
Fissile laughed about that for days.
He smiled like a father at the team, "I'm proud of you all. You've accomplished so much. It's funny, Phase One on Earth will probably never be complete. Phase Two on the Moon has really just started, and Phase Three on Mars will begin soon. And yet it seems like we'll always yearn for more, to continue to seek beyond the horizon. I wonder what's in store for you next?"
Neil looked at Fissile, "Well, next we have to be on stage. But for next summer we have a few cool ideas that we'll discuss with you after the show." He gave Fissile a hug, "Thanks for the gig."
Everyone else gave Fissile a hug.
Fissile held up his hand to hold them up for just a moment. "This is your first night. Don't be nervous. Think of it as a science experiment. You don't have to be perfect the first time. Remember the Joe Walsh classic 'Funk 49'? Funk 1 through Funk 48, not so good. But Funk 49 was perfect. Not to worry. Go have fun."

Woody came over, "OK, you're up, I'll go introduce you."

They heard Woody say, "And now, fresh from their gig on the Moon, give it up for Sci Crew."

The crowd had heard some demo material from the Club's web site and were appreciative in their applause.

They ran out on stage, where Neil and Anne strapped on their guitars, Yang jumped behind his drum set, and Ellie sat down behind her organ. Mae took the microphone from Woody and looked out into the crowd.

"Thank you. Our first song is sort of a spin on a tune from an old classic movie. We call it "Somewhere Over the Horizon," and it goes something like this…"

www.ingramcontent.com/pod-product-compliance
Lightning Source LLC
Chambersburg PA
CBHW060142130626
46556CB00006B/2460